The Recipe Of A Godly Woman IV

Perfection

LaToya Geter

Re'Nique Publishing

Copyright © 2022 LaToya Geter

All Rights Reserved. No parts of this book shall be duplicated, distributed, reproduced, or photocopied without permission from the author. This is a work of fiction. All characters, events, incidents, and places are from the author's imagination. The characters are not based upon actual persons, living or dead. The resemblance of actual persons living or dead is coincidental.

I dedicate this book to readers who continue to support the series. I also dedicate this book to mothers who are struggling with caring for children who are living with trauma.

Audrey

My home of Crestview was not just any ole city. It was now a prospering city. I was proud of the work my husband and other prominent figures were doing in the city. I was grateful to be his wife! I was still by his side, blessed to be a part of the change. The sides were still different, but some things had changed. The rich and uppity on the east side were helping the trying individuals on the west side. Helping included opening support centers and other services for individuals in need. My husband joined the cause. He served as a counselor for individuals in need.

Outside in the backyard of our home, my husband built a reading nook for me. I loved it. I enjoyed sitting under the shaded trees on the comfortable furry cushions as I read many suspense novels. It was rather relaxing after work.

His presence coming out of our home through the patio caught my attention. I smiled at him before I noticed he was not smiling. His look of concern caused me to ease up from reading. He placed his hands in his pocket while walking over to me. He sat down next to me and sighed. I knew my husband. He had something to tell me.

"Just tell me," I said.

"You should call Kim."

There was no need to call her. My circle of friends was too close not to be by one another's side in times of turmoil. I picked up my phone on the small table next to the nook. I called Allison and Lauren and told them we needed to check on Kim. Calling her was not an option.

My husband would not tell me what was wrong. All he said was Kim was coming to him for counseling. She had no idea he was going to be her counselor.

Allison and Lauren stood behind me as I knocked on Kim's front door. After I knocked three sets of four knocks with no answer, it was time for Allison to use her spare key. The house was dark. I flipped a nearby switch. We could not believe our eyes. Shattered plant vases were on the floor. Family pictures of her twin daughters, husband, and herself were barely hanging on the wall. Glass scattered on the floor caused us to move carefully through the area. We found her sitting on her couch in tears. Allison rushed over to her. She fell into her best friend's arms, sobbing.

"Talk to us," pleaded Allison. "What happened here?"

"Daniel has a referral for you to see him for counseling," I said. "He did not tell me why. He felt we should check on you."

"Where are the girls?" asked Allison

"The hospital," cried Kim.

"What?" asked Allison. "Why? Where is Derrick?"

"On his way to rot in hell. First, he has to serve time for what he did to my babies."

Kim

I walked into the small room with light blue painted walls. Three other women were sitting in a circle of six chairs.

"Hello," I said, filling seat number four.

They each spoke before we sat in silence. A few minutes later, another woman came into the room. She joined the circle. I did not catch her name. I don't think I was trying to catch her name. I was only there because I was court-ordered to be. I was not trying to make friends. An African American man walked in. I knew he was the facilitator. I was trying to figure out how he would lead a support group full of women. He sat down in chair number six. He was not the facilitator. I did not pay any attention to him. Where was the facilitator? I was ready to go, and the session had not even started.

A woman in a blue blouse and fitted black skirt walked into the room carrying a bag. She was the facilitator. We started the support group by introducing ourselves. I still did not catch everyone's name. I barely said mine. She gave the rules of the group. A bunch of talk about confidentiality, and then she let us go.

I pushed the hospital door open to find my baby girl still on oxygen. The respirator was helping her breathe. The lines on the machine were active; she was living. I would never have imagined my child fighting for her life because of an overdose. I had been coming to see her for a month now. She had not said a word. Her eyes had not opened. I was hurting. I pulled the chair up, sitting beside the hospital bed daily. I buried my head in the hospital bed. I did not try to fight the tears.

Tillman Mental Health Facility's visiting hours were noon until six o' clock in the evening on Saturdays. Every Saturday for a month, I visited my other daughter. The plan was to visit her every Saturday until she was well enough to come home. On one visit, I could not see her. The facility took her visitation because she was on a suicide watch. She attempted to commit suicide again. A suicide attempt is what got her admitted. Her sister swallowed two bottles of pills, and she slit her arms. There were cuts from her wrists up to her shoulders. I had no words for the man that came to the visitation room to give me the news. My tears spoke for me. I did not even say thank you. I got up from the table and left the room.

Will

Was I having another nightmare? Yes! Screams traveled through my ears, causing me to wake up. I sat straight up in bed. I threw the covers from my body. I rushed into my daughter's room. I saw her tossing, turning, and fighting. That was the nightmare I had been living with for six months. I sat on the edge of her bed, trying to wake her up.

"Ryleigh! Wake up, baby girl," I said, holding her to keep her still. That was tough. Even though she was eight years old, she was strong. Over the years of living with her mother and stepfather, she taught herself to be tough.

"She's having another one," my son said, standing in the doorway of her room.

"Junior. I need you to stay calm. Go back to your room, okay."

"I should've killed them!" he yelled as his anger began to build.

I had to think of something to help him calm down. He loved his little sister.

"Junior, how about you help me with your sister?"

My son came over to the other side of her bed.

He kissed her on her forehead. She slowly opened her eyes. She was shaking and breathing heavily.

"Daddy!" she cried.

"I'm here, sweetheart." I held her close. She wrapped her arms around me, holding on tight. I pulled my son into my arms.

"Come on," I said to them, getting out of bed with my daughter in my arms. She wrapped her arms around my neck and rested her head on my shoulder as we walked to my bedroom. I walked into my room and placed her in my bed. I got into bed, and Ryleigh snuggled up with me. Junior got into bed with us. I stayed up staring at the ceiling as long as I could. I wanted a trauma-free life for my children. Before I knew it, I found myself falling asleep.

The sun woke me the next time and not the screams of my daughter. She was fine. Sleeping with me always helped her feel better. On the other side of me was my son. Being in my presence always helped ease his anger.

Kim

The question, "Kim, would you like to share?" interrupted my zoned-out thoughts. I did not know what she wanted me to share. Even if I did have something to share, I didn't care to share. I eyed her. The facilitator tried to act like she was addressing the group, but I knew she was talking about me when she said, "You all must participate for me to give the judge a good report." After her subliminal statement, I felt like sharing.

"I don't care about a good report." I did not yell. I did not have the energy. "I don't think any of us care about a good report. You're the specialist; do you think we care about a good report?"

"You are here," she said. "I think you care."

"I care about my children," I snapped. "I am attending because they need help. I need to know how to handle them when they come home."

"You have to be mentally stable as well," she replied.

I rolled my eyes at her. She smiled at me and said to the group, "I will place you all into pairs. As you deal with your children, some individuals may not understand what you are experiencing with your child or going to experience. It's always good to have support. When your children are having episodes or acting out, you may forget what we discuss here. It's normal. You all are human. You will need help. My goal for the pairs is for you all to get to know one another's story and support one another."

My friends and pastor supported me. I didn't need any support. Especially not from women who were born and raised in Crestview or outsiders. The town was now a city, but that did not mean the gossipers matured into saints. It did not mean that new gossipers had not made Crestview their home.

"Kim and Will, you two will be support partners."

Furthermore, just because he was a man did not mean he was not a gossiper. I wasn't even going to allow myself to trust him.

Will

Did I have to be paired with her? She could have placed me with any other group member. I would have been fine! Kim didn't even talk in the group! I knew she wasn't going to speak in the pair! I wanted help with my children! I wanted to be able to help them deal with their issues. I didn't feel she would be a good support partner. I decided to try it, even though I knew she wouldn't cooperate.

"You all already know one another," said the facilitator. "I want you all to take this time to find out how you can be supportive. You can't fully be a support system if you all do not know things about each other. You may find some of these things can help the person with whatever is they are dealing with."

I decided to let Kim start. "Ladies first," I smiled. She did not smile back. That corny smile failed!

"You aren't from here," she said.

She was right, but I was expecting her to tell me about herself! Since she was talking, I went with it. Maybe it could lead to her sharing information about herself.

"I am not," I smiled.

"NOLA, perhaps?"

"Correct."

"What brings you to Crestview?"

"Life."

"She said we have to explain."

If she wanted me to talk, she would have to say more. "Well, if I explain that to you, you will have to explain why you are here. I do not think you want to do that. You barely participate in the regular group."

"Yeah, you are right about that," she said, rolling her eyes. "I don't trust anybody from Crestview or people that live in Crestview."

"I have been here for six months. I have not had a bad experience."

"Keep living here," she smirked.

"Can you tell me about Crestview? Please, positive things only. We are already here in group therapy. I do not want to know the negative things."

"Oh! Don't worry. They will come to you!"

"I will deal with them if they do."

"About the positive things…."

Talking about the positive things about her hometown seemed to help her loosen up. She even smiled. That was a good sign. At least I knew she could smile. We were approaching month 2 of the support group, and she never laughed at a joke or funny story. She always sat in her chair with a blank stare.

I needed to ask her a question. I was hoping that she would not get offended. Her demeanor said she did not go. I did not know where the question would lead the conversation. If she did not go, I knew she still knew of one. I avoided the question and made a statement. "I need to find a church to attend."

"There are several nice churches around here," she said.

"I drove past some. I told myself I would visit one. My kids keep me busy. I need to stop making excuses."

"Temple of Heaven is a good one," she said.

The following Sunday, I took my kids to church. We enjoyed the service. Back home, I would take them to church on the weekends they would visit. We had not been to church since we moved to Crestview. It was a joy to see Ryleigh and Junior praising the Lord their way.

After the service, two small girls rushed over to us. I watched as they introduced themselves to Ryleigh.

"Hi! My name is Ariel!"

"Hi, I am Layla!"

My daughter was a bit shy. She twisted in her dress, waving at the girls.

"We saw you when my mama asked the new people to stand up," said Layla.

"What is your name?" asked Ariel.

Ryleigh looked at me for reassurance to tell them her name. I smiled with a nod. She quietly introduced herself.

"Nice to meet you, Ryleigh," smiled Ariel.

"We are eight!" smiled Layla, "How old are you?"

"I'm eight," said Ryleigh.

"I haven't seen you at school," said Layla.

"She probably goes to the other school," said Ariel.

The duo was rather cute and entertaining. The pastor of the church then made his way over. He extended his hand to shake mine,

"Pastor Daniel Reynolds," he said. "I see you have met my daughter and niece."

"Daddy, her name is Ryleigh!" smiled Ariel. "She is eight! Like us!"

"Will Evans," I said, introducing myself. "This is my son Will Evans Jr."

Pastor Reynolds shook my son's hand. "Nice to meet you all. Welcome to Temple of Heaven."

A woman dressed in a purple dress with silver heels and a low bun with pearls approached us.

"Mama! I met Ryleigh," said Ariel.

"Oh good!" smiled the first lady as she extended her hand to introduce herself.

I expected to meet the pastor and first lady. I did not know what to expect from them. Everyone has their opinion about how the pastor and first lady are supposed to present themselves. The couple met those expectations and more. They were very genuine. They laughed, joked, and we even exchanged phone numbers for our girls to play with one another. We enjoyed our time at the church. The positive atmosphere helped me. I was going to attend church again.

Kim

My girls were much older than my nieces Ariel and Layla. They were their babysitters. Since my girls were away, I spent much time with my friends and their families. It would help me get my mind off my girls. Being alone was not good for me. I was alone at home when Audrey called and invited me to a day at the park.

Crestview East Park was now Unity Park East, thanks to the work of Daniel and Audrey. The newly renovated Crestview West Park was Unity Park West. I pulled onto the parking lot of Unity Park East. There were several cars. I recognized the cars. One belonged to Lauren. Allison was there. Daniel's black Denali was parked.

A small girl was playing with Ariel and Layla on the playground. I was confused as I only saw my friends at a nearby pavilion. Lauren had a son and two daughters, Layla, Lil Greg, and baby Cassidy. Allison only had an adopted son, Jake. He and Lil Greg were roller blading together down the sidewalk.

"Hey, girl," said Allison as I approached the pavilion.

"Hey, y'all!" I said, speaking to everyone.

Daniel had the grill smelling good. Lauren and her husband, Cornelius, were enjoying a game of spades with Allison and her husband, Jeffery. I sat down, picking up the pen to take score.

"Allison! Jeff! Y'all done got set twice! I taught y'all better than that!"

Allison laughed, "Leave us alone!"

"You didn't teach her that good!" laughed Lauren.

"Imma let them lose. Me and Audrey will get on this and make y'all get up! I said to Lauren.

"Girl, get out of here. Stop fooling yourself!" laughed Lauren

"That is what I am going to be saying to you!" I said.

The small girls then came to the table. "Mama, is her daddy back with her swimsuit? We want to play in the water falls and sprinklers?" asked Layla.

"I am right here," he said.

I could not believe whose voice I was hearing! I quickly turned around! Will stopped in mid-stride. We both made eye contact! Awkward! Why was my support partner at the park with my friends?

"Um, y'all know each other?" asked Cornelius.

My friends knew I had to attend group counseling. I did not know what all he told them. I was not about to put his business out there.

"We do," he said. "Kim told me about your church."

"Hi, Will," I said.

"How are you?" he asked me.

"I'm good," I said.

"Let's get you changed," he said to the small girl.

He headed to the bathroom with his daughter.

Audrey had to ask. "How do you know Will?"

"I can't say," I said, hoping she would get the hint.

"Oh!" said Allison. "So he attends group counseling with you?"

I could have punched Allison. Lauren laughed. Audrey shook her head.

"I want to dye your hair brunette or a brown color," I laughed.

"Don't start!" laughed Allison, flipping her long blonde hair.

"He has been coming to church," said Daniel.

"That is good." I smiled, "Leave me out of the equation right now, please."

"I wasn't going to say anything," said Daniel.

"Thanks. Leave it for my session, doc!"

Daniel laughed. "I'm nowhere near you or Cornelius's status."

"Speaking of that," said Cornelius. "I had one of your patients in the emergency room. Has her mom brought her in for a check-up?"

"Yes, I got her file. The mom brought her to see me. The little girl is doing better," I said.

Will made his way back to the pavilion. He sat down at the table across from me.

"Y'all still getting whooped?" he laughed.

"They getting to' up!" laughed Cornelius.

"This is the last game! Looks like y'all about to get set again!" laughed Lauren.

"Three times," laughed Will.

"I want to see you on the table!" laughed Jeffery. "Cause' you been talking since you got here!"

"I'm ready! As soon as Daniel is off the grill," said Will.

Daniel then said, "Play with Kim. It's going to be a minute."

This man had the nerve to look at me and ask, "Can you play? I do not lose!"

Who was he talking to? I was the queen of spades! He didn't even know, but he was about to find out!

Will

She was a beast at spades! I didn't even know it! It didn't matter how her cards fell! She still played her hand! Lauren and Cornelius were losing! They were not doing too much talking either! Kim, on the other hand, was talking mad cash! She was a character!

I dealt the cards for our final hand. Kim placed her hand how she wanted.

"We have won," she said. "Do you all want to play this hand?"

"We see the score," laughed Lauren, "Yeah, we are playing this out."

Kim smirked. "Suit yourself! I was trying to help you out! Losing is not the same as getting taxed! Which is what I am about to do with this hand! Tax y'all!"

I laughed, and she said, "My partner must have something!"

I kept laughing. "I know we won. Cornelius and Lauren are supposed to bid first. They don't need to bid the way my hand is and how you been playing!"

Kim laughed. "Sounds like you're saying we can save them the trouble of bidding their sad hands. We got a ten hand!"

"I couldn't have said it any better," I laughed.

Cornelius laughed. "Y'all talking across the board!"

"Game hasn't started, patna!" laughed Kim.

Who was this sitting across the table from me? She was not the Kim who was at group counseling sessions. I liked this, Kim!

My day at the clinic was going well. I finished shots with a regular patient. I headed toward the nurse's station. My PA handed me a file.

"New patient," she said. "Eight-year-old girl has symptoms of chicken pox."

"Ewww," I said, thinking back to when my girls caught them.

I took the chart and headed back to my office. I reviewed the chart before going into the room. After reading all the documents, I was ready to work my magic to help the little person feel better. With all new patients, I took Yaya with me. Yaya was a puppet lamb I used to help my new patients who may have been afraid or nervous.

I knocked on the door. I then opened it and stuck my hand in with Yaya. I moved the puppet around. I could hear the little girl laughing.

"Is someone in the room itchy?" asked Yaya.

The little girl said, "Yes. It stings too."

"Hmmm.." said Yaya, "I will let the Dr. know that. My name is Yaya. What is your name?"

"Ryleigh," she said.

"Nice to meet you, Ryleigh. Do you want to talk to me more, or can I get Dr. Kim?" asked Yaya.

Ryleigh laughed. "You can go get Dr. Kim!"

"Okay! Bye, bye Ryleigh. See you next time! I hope you feel better."

"Bye-bye, Yaya," laughed Ryleigh.

I pulled my hand back out of the door. My nurses were smiling. I smiled at them before taking the puppet back to my office. I opened the door to the room. I stopped in mid-stride.

Will and I made direct eye contact. I recognized the little girl. I did not catch her name the day at the park. His little girl Ryleigh was there to see me for chicken pox.

"Hey, Kim," he said.

"Hey, Will," I said.

"She started itching yesterday morning. It got worse last night. This morning she was so irritated."

"I am sorry!" I said to him. I then said to Ryleigh, "Yaya told me you were itching. She said the bumps burned."

"They do," she said to me.

"Well, you do have chicken pox. It has been going around. Someone at school must have returned without being completely treated." I then said to Will, "I will give her a prescription. You can always use the old remedy of calamine lotion as well."

"Thank you," he said.

"You're welcome," I smiled.

"Are you going to be my new doctor?" asked Ryleigh.

"Sure thing, kiddo!" I smiled.

I wrote the prescription and gave the information to a nurse to take to the room. There was a knock at my office door. It was the same nurse. "The father of Ryleigh Evans would like to see you." I was confused. Did he have a question? I told her to send him back. Will walked into my office alone.

"I need to ask you a question. I did not want to ask in front of Ryleigh."

"Okay, what can I help you with?"

"She had a primary care physician who was writing her referrals back home. I need a new physician for her. She needs an updated referral for *mental health counseling.*"

"I am always open for new patients," I said. "We can start her check-ups. Make an appointment with the receptionist in the waiting room before you leave."

"Will do," said Will. "Thank you again."

"You're welcome," I said as he left my office.

Will

I was grateful Kim was willing to be Ryleigh's primary care physician. She did help us. She began to do check-ups for Ryleigh and my son. She completed referrals for them to continue receiving counseling in Crestview since they had not been since we left home.

Kim was a good doctor. She talked more during appointments than she did at the support group. I hoped our parent-and-doctor relationship would help us during our group session. I was ready to go to the next session to see how much progress we would make.

At the next session, I was sitting at our assigned table. The group session was about to start. Kim had not made it. She walked in as we were about to break into our support groups. She did not look well at all. I did not know her that well. The bags under her eyes said she was extremely tired or was crying. She plopped down in the chair in front of me at the table.

"Hey," I said.

"Hi," said Kim.

There was that Kim! The Kim who was not at the park and the one who was not at her clinic! Like always, I started our conversation.

"I guess you didn't have a good day."

"Why do you think that?" she asked me.

"I've seen you in a good mood. Your mood is off today."

"My day is not up for discussion."

"What is? You don't like to talk," I said.

Kim rolled her eyes at me. She leaned back in the chair and stared at me.

Her mood sucked all the excitement out of me that I had before I got to the session. I did the same as she did. I threw myself back in the chair and stared back at her.

That same night, I was asleep in my bed. I felt someone patting me. I opened my eyes to see my daughter. I sat up in bed. She was crying. I picked her up, sitting her in bed with me. She snuggled up against me.

"What's wrong, baby girl?" I asked her.

"I had a bad dream," she cried.

"I am so sorry," I said to her. "Daddy will make it better. I will stay up with you until you can go back to sleep."

"Can we call my friends Ariel and Layla?" she asked.

It was two in the morning. Of course, she could not call them. She then said to me,

"I wish Yaya was real."

I then thought back to Kim using Yaya at every doctor visit.

Kim

My phone started to ring. The nightmare about the phone call I received when my daughter was found in the locker room at school overdosed on pills was beginning. It was an event that I was constantly reliving in my sleep. One that was worse each time. The phone kept ringing. I realized my phone was actually ringing. I cut on the lamp that sat on my nightstand next to my bed. The phone read Will. He must have needed support. As much as I did not want to answer the phone, I knew answering was the right thing to do.

"Hey," he said. "I know it's late. Ryleigh had a nightmare. She seems to be fond of Yaya. Maybe you can help her calm down."

I smiled at the thought of his little girl. I was glad I answered his call. "Yes, sure I will," I said.

Yaya did help Ryleigh calm down. After their talk, she was ready to go back to bed in her room like a big girl.

"Thank you," said Will.

"You're welcome," I said. I had to ask how he was. I viewed the child's file multiple times as her primary care physician. I knew things were hard on him.

THE RECIPE OF A GODLY WOMAN IV

"I am making it," he said, "Since they both have started therapy here, they seem to be doing a little better. So, I am better."

"That is good," I said to him.

"How are you?" he asked me, "I do not think it is fair that you know what is going on with my children, and you won't tell me anything about your girls."

"I am their PCP," I said.

"You're my support partner," he said to me, "I can't support you if I do not know. I feel I owe you. Especially for tonight."

"You do not owe me," I said, "It's all good. I am glad I could help".

"I know you are not going to talk to me about your girls. How about lunch on me tomorrow?"

"I am okay. I promise I am. I'm going to get some sleep. I'll see you at the session tomorrow."

The next day I was headed out of my office for lunch. As I was walking out, my receptionist was walking in with lunch. Was she carrying my favorite? I recognized the Italian Bistro bag.

"It was delivered," she said.

"Thank you," I said, taking the bag and walking back over to my desk.

I sat down as my cell phone rang. I did not even bother to look to see who was calling as I opened the bag.

"Hello," I said.

"My Uber eats notification said your lunch was delivered," said Will.

I took the phone from my ear, put it on speaker, placed in on my desk, sat down, and stared at it before I said anything.

"It was," I said. "Thank you, but you don't owe me."

"I do," he said, "You told me about the church, you helped me with my children, and you answered your phone at two in the morning to support me. Plus, I will always be your spades partner when we hang out".

I laughed at the last part.

"I hope you enjoy it, and I hope you have a great rest of the day," he said before the phone call ended.

Lunch was delicious! It was my favorite! I was interested as to how he knew I loved the Italian-styled stuffed bell peppers.

Before the group session, I went to the hospital to visit my daughter. She still was not responding. She was still alive. I placed a card on her window seal. I took the deflated pink balloons, her favorite color, and replaced them with new ones. I sat with her for as long as I could. I couldn't miss the group session. The entire time I cried. I wanted my baby to open her eyes. I wanted both of my girls to come home.

Before leaving the hospital, I kissed my girl on her forehead. I wiped my tears as I left the room. The ride down the elevator was slow. The drive to the group session was even slower. I parked my car in the parking lot, forced myself out

THE RECIPE OF A GODLY WOMAN IV

of the car, and begged my legs to get me inside. Will was already at the table. I eased into the seat in front of him. Will was anxious to talk like always once we broke off into pairs. I was ready to go home, turn my lights off in my bedroom and lock myself in my room.

The following Saturday, I went to see my daughter. She was not on suicidal watch. She could have visitors. I was happy about that. I sat in the family room at a table. She walked in and plopped down in the seat. She held her head down.

"Hey baby," I said to her.

She did not respond to me.

"I came to see you. I visit your sister too. She is doing well. She still isn't responding."

My daughter only held her head down. Throughout the entire visit, she did not raise her head. I only looked at her long black hair draped down the side of her face. She did not say two words to me.

Seeing her depressed and sad hurt me. Tears were ready to fall from my eyes and down my face. I held them tight. I did not want to cry in front of my baby. I was weak, but I knew I needed to be strong for her and her sister.

Will

The Reynolds invited me over for a game night. I decided I would go and bring the kids. I was looking forward to the game of spades again. It was fun the last time. My children and I walked into their home. Ryleigh and Junior both took off to find the other children. I noticed everyone was in the dining room. They were eating finger food. Kim was not there. Audrey was headed to the fridge when I asked her where she was.

"She was not feeling it tonight," she said to me.

I thought about her mood at our last session. I decided to reach out to her. After all, I was her support partner. She did not answer the first time I called. I decided to call a second time. She answered,

"I don't feel like coming," she said.

I laughed. "How did you know I was calling about that?"

"I'm quite sure Daniel invited you. You suck without me in spades." she laughed.

"Woah! Don't get beside yourself, ma'am. I'm good without you."

"Yeah, yeah," she laughed.

I told her the real reason for calling her. I was worried about her. I wanted to make sure she was okay.

"I'll be fine," she said.

"Sounds like you want to talk," I said to her.

"I will talk in the group," she said.

"No, you won't," I said.

"Yes, I will," she sighed.

"How about you come over here to the game night? It will help you feel better, or I can come to your place, and you won't have a choice but to talk."

She smirked. "You don't even know where I live."

"I bet I can find out," I said. "All your friends know where you live."

"You are not a friend. They do not know you that well to tell you."

"I have been around long enough," I said. "One will definitely tell me."

"I bet!" she smirked. "Must be the same one who told you about my favorite dish from Italian Bistro!"

I had to laugh. Her friends didn't tell me. I found out on my own.

"I shall not reveal my source," I said.

She laughed, and I could hear her yawn.

"Sounds like you're in bed. Get up and put some clothes on. I will give you thirty minutes. If you are not here, I will be at your front door."

"Boy, bye!" she said, hanging up in my face.

Thirty minutes later, the doorbell rang. Audrey looked at Daniel. He shrugged his shoulders. I then knew it was my cue to let them know I would get the door.

"I'll get it," I said, getting up from their couch in the middle of our charades game.

I opened their door to find Kim standing on the other side in a hoodie and jeans with her Nikes.

Kim

Will was standing there cheesing like a kid on Easter, waiting on their basket. I pushed him out of the way.

"Let me find out you over here getting smacked in spades," I said.

"We haven't started yet," he said. "I was waiting on you."

I walked into the dining room area. All of them had the nerve to start clapping. I wanted to punch all of them in the face. I turned to Will and pushed him again. "Did you tell them I was coming?" He held his hands up, laughing. I then turned to my friends. Audrey eyed me. Lauren folded her arms, and Allison was too busy giggling.

"He did not tell us anything," said Lauren, "Is there something you want to tell us?"

"Are you trying to be funny?" I laughed.

Lauren shrugged her shoulders. She was making me think she was behind him bringing my favorite for lunch. Audrey was always lost! I ruled her out a long time ago. Allison then said, "We are just happy you came!" I eyed her. She could have been the culprit.

We played spades. The women partnered

with the men, which was kind of awkward for Will and me since we were not a couple. The odd balls did beat every couple.

Once the dining area house was clean, we all began to head out. "I'll see you all later," I said. "It was fun."

"Bye, girl," said Allison, running to give me a hug. I hugged the others.

"I'll walk you out," I heard Will say.

I turned around to see him coming out of the den behind me. I did not need this man walking me to my car. I knew I would not hear the end of it if I put up a fuss.

The lights of my white Audi lit as I unlocked it with my switch.

"I see you, Doc," he said.

I laughed. I then saw lights flash on the red Camaro.

"I knew that was yours," I laughed, "I see you."

"I am an engineering manager," he said.

"I see you mister engineering manager," I said, leaning against my Audi. "Is that what brought you to Crestview?"

"Life did," he said again. *I remember him saying that at the group session.*

"Are you ever going to explain that?" I asked him.

"Are you going to explain why you do not cooperate in the group session? Are you going to explain why you were not going to come tonight?" he asked me.

I rolled my eyes. I folded my arms. I tapped my foot. I already told him on the phone I would talk at the group session. *Why was he pressing the issue?*

"I will explain at the group session." I sighed.

"I will, too," he said.

Will

Just as I expected, she didn't talk at the next group session! She just sat in the chair! I was heated! I did not talk either! We were so unproductive! Other groups were talking! The facilitator noticed. She pulled up a chair and sat down. Kim rolled her eyes. She then snatched her purse before she stormed out of the room.

"I would like a new partner," I said to the facilitator. Her name was Jillian.

Jillian then said, "I know she is a difficult support partner. I paired you all with people for a reason. I can't tell you what is going on with her. I want you to know you all can help one another."

"I can't help her if she does not talk!" I yelled.

"Calm down," said Jillian. "Have you learned anything about her? Try to use that to help."

"Is her behavior going to affect my court situation?" I asked her.

"It will not," she smiled. "You are doing a good job."

"You said we are supposed to be gathering information to present at the end of the group session. I do not have any information about her," I said.

"Keep trying," she said. "I know there is something you can use. This project is to help you deal with tough spots you reach when living with your children as well."

Jillian got up from the table. She gave me a pat on the back. She was encouraging. My partner was not. I placed my forehead in the palm of my mind. I had to think of a way to get information about Kim.

As I was driving home from the session, I thought about Ryleigh and her relationship with Kim that developed over the months since she became her physician. I did not want to use my child, but I needed to use my child to make sure I could keep my children. I knew Jillian said I would not lose them. I wanted to make sure. I had to know they would not be placed back with their mother. After thinking long and hard, I decided to do a little more research.

Kim

It hurt for my daughter not to talk to me, but I still drove every weekend to see her. It was not her fault. My phone began to ring as I drove. I saw Will's number pop up on the car screen. I didn't want to take the call. I knew why he was calling. I decided to answer.

"What's up, Will?

"How are you?" he asked me.

"I'm okay, and yourself?"

"I'm doing better."

"Get to the point. I know you are calling because I left the group."

"I am not calling about that."

` "Well, what's up?"

"What are you doing later?"

"Depends on how this visit goes," I said without thinking.

"A visit?" he asked me.

I hurried and lied about an incoming call. He brought it. I quickly hung up the phone.

This visit was different. No, my daughter did not talk. She wore her hair in a ponytail, pulled out of her face. I sat with her for about two hours before heading back home. Like every visit, the ride back home was full of tears. My phone rang. My car informed me that Will was calling. I hit the answer button on the car screen.

"Hello," I said, wiping my tears.

"Hey. You didn't call me back."

"I was busy."

"At the visit," he said. "Yeah, I know."

I knew one of my friends had to tell him! I was angry! I did not want them telling him anything!

"Okay! Which one told you I was visiting my daughter at the mental health facility?" I yelled.

"No one did," he calmly said.

"Yes, they did!" I yelled.

"Sounds like you're crying," he said. "Where are you?"

I hung the phone up in his face. I found myself crying in bed after every visit on a Saturday with my daughter. I did not want to answer my phone or my door. I locked myself in my house and cried myself to sleep.

I woke up to Allison shaking me. Audrey and Lauren were standing with her. I pulled the cover over my head. I did not want to talk to them. Allison pulled the cover back down.

"You didn't have a good visit today," she said.

"Nope! Now that is something else one of you can tell Will."

They each looked at one another in confusion.

"We have not told Will anything," said

Allison.

"How did he know about the visit?" I snapped.

"He called Daniel," said Audrey. "You told him. He said he talked to you, and you mentioned a visit. He said he was worried about you because you did not sound good on the phone."

I covered my face. "I did tell him! Ugh! I wasn't trying to tell him! It came out!"

"Why is that a bad thing?" asked Allison

"Nothing," I said.

"We are having dinner at our house later," said Audrey.

"You need to be there," said Allison.

"We know you haven't had anything to eat," said Lauren. "Don't make us come back over here."

"Alright!" I snapped.

I promised my friends I would get out of bed. I told them I would meet them at dinner. I broke that promise! I stayed in bed! I missed the dinner date!

I heard my phone ring while I slept under my covers. I threw my covers back and snatched my phone from my nightstand without looking at it. I knew it was one of them calling because I missed the dinner date!

"What?" I snapped.

"Hello to you too," said Will.

My eyes bucked! Why was he calling me? What did he want?

"You missed dinner with us," he said.

"Yeah, so, now what?" I snapped.

"Come out and have dessert with me."

I was quiet on the phone. Dessert was my favorite portion of the meal! How did he know that if none of my friends were telling him things?

"Chocolate ice cream," he said. "I'll meet you at the café on the west side."

The chocolate ice cream made from scratch by the west side café was the bomb! It was my favorite! With the mood I was in, I could not say no. It would probably help me feel better.

Will

The west side café was pretty empty. It was nine. They were closing at eleven. I sat in a booth. I tapped on the table that held two cups of chocolate ice cream. My thoughts were telling me Kim was going to stand me up. The door bell sounded as she walked into the café. She looked comfy! Her hair sat in a messy bun. She wore a pair of black leggings and a red hoodie. She sat down in the booth.

"For you," I said, sliding the ice cream over to her.

"Thank you, but you did not have to," she said.

"You're welcome," I said.

"I guess it's time for me to talk since I let the mental health facility visit slip out."

"Only if you want to," he said. "Ryleigh asked about you. She made me think about it earlier. I wanted to make sure you were okay."

She smiled. "Thank you. How is she?"

"She is doing fine," I said. "As sweet as she can be."

She began to stare off into space as we talked about Ryleigh. I thought she tuned me out for a

THE RECIPE OF A GODLY WOMAN IV

second.

"I have two daughters," she said to me.

Her twins were Mia and Mya. She loved them with all she had. She would move mountains for them. She remembered the day she found out she was pregnant. She was happy. Her husband was happy. When the doctor saw the twins, they were overjoyed. They arrived healthy and on time! *They were perfect*! They started pulling up and walking early! They were perfect! Complete sentences by age two. They were perfect! No struggling with bottles, pacifiers, or the potty. They were perfect! In preschool, they learned quickly. They were perfect! Elementary school, you know, they had straight A's! No, write-ups. No detention! They were perfect! Jr. high school, they loved it! One found a niche for cheering, and the other loved to dance. Those grades didn't drop! They were her perfect pre-teens.

She lit up when she talked about her girls. I wanted her to keep talking, but she stopped. I watched as she lowered her head.

"Are you okay?" I asked her.

Her eyes filled with tears, "Excuse me," she said, getting up from the table. She went into the bathroom. Minutes later, she came back to the table.

"Enough about my girls," she said. "I hope this does not sound unprofessional. I looked at your kid's file, of course. Are you really a single dad caring for them?"

"I am," I said.

"Fighting for custody...." she said.

"That too. Praying every day that when that time comes, the judge will give me full custody."

"I see you with them at the doctor visits. They love you. You are doing a great job."

"Thank you," I said to her. "You mentioned your husband. Are you married?"

"I was married," she said. I wanted to know more. Instead, she quickly switched the topic.

"If you do not mind me asking, what happened with you and their mother?"

I smiled because I was nervous. I never liked discussing what happened in my previous relationship.

"She wanted a different type of life. I pursued her. The whole time I thought she would change. She did not. I kept trying. The kids came along. We got married. I think she did that because her mother and family kept telling her it was the right thing, but she was not feeling a marriage. I should have known after proposing. She pushed the wedding back. I loved her. I had to learn the hard way."

"I am sorry," she said. "I am also sorry about what happened to your children."

I knew she was going to read the entire file on my children. She was their doctor. They did not deserve what happened. I made a promise to them that I was not going to allow it to happen again. I meant it too.

"Thank you," I said.

She smiled at me. I had to ask how her ice cream was. It was gone! She laughed and said, "It was good! Thank you."

I suggested that we meet at the café once a week. I figured it would help us get through the group session. She smiled and said, "That is a good idea."

Kim

He smiled at me. He probably thought I was going to object. I thought about it, but our conversation was helpful. I left the café in a better mood. He bugged me about calling him when I made it home. I guessed he was worried about me since I had a habit of not showing up to events or always being so angry and sad. I told him I would. I called when I pulled into my driveway. I thought our conversation was going to be brief. It was not! I found myself talking to him as I kicked off my shoes. I made my way upstairs to my bedroom. I plopped down on my bed and stretched out. Before I knew it, we were talking about sports. He was surprised that I had a favorite team. He was even more surprised when I told him I enjoyed basketball more than football. He was a fan of basketball too.

"Your team is going to lose to us this year!" he said.

"Dude, you're out of your mind!" I laughed. "They are not!"

Sports led to my favorite food. His favorite food was chicken and dumplings.

"Can you make some?" he asked me.

THE RECIPE OF A GODLY WOMAN IV

"Down home cooking! I'll make them from scratch!" I said, bragging.

"Girl, you can't cook!" he laughed.

I heard a small voice ask, "Daddy! Who is that?"

"Why aren't you sleeping, baby girl?" he asked Ryleigh.

"Bad dream," she said.

He started to facetime me. My heart dropped. I answered it off impulse. He and Ryleigh were looking at me. She smiled from ear to ear.

"Hey, Dr. Kim!"

"Hey, sweet girl!"

"What are you doing?"

"About to beat your daddy up because he said I can't cook!"

Ryleigh laughed. "Our favorite food is chicken and dumplings! Can you make some?"

Before I could answer, I heard Junior in the background.

"Who is that, Daddy? Sounds like Dr. Kim!"

"Everybody is up over there," I laughed.

"They are wide awake!" he laughed.

I could see junior flopping down on the bed. He stuck his head in front of Will.

"That is, you, Dr. Kim! Hey!"

"Hey, Junior," I laughed.

"I heard y'all talking about chicken and dumplings," he said, "Only my GG makes the best ones!"

Will laughed, "Dr. Kim said she can cook

47

better than your GG."

"I did not," I laughed.

Junior said, "Daddy doesn't even know how to cook!"

I was cracking up, and so was Will.

"So, you throw yo pops under the bus like that."

"Dr. Kim! We be starving!" laughed Ryleigh.

Will then said, "Since y'all are starving, why don't you go let Dr. Kim feed you!"

"Daddy, we all need to go, cause you need to eat too! You know you don't like your own cooking!" laughed Junior.

"Can we come to your house Dr. Kim?" asked Ryleigh.

Lord! The baby put me on the spot! I wasn't prepared for that at all.

"Um, sure," I said.

"You are going to cook chicken and dumplings, right?" asked Junior.

"I am," I laughed.

"Yep! We are coming!" he laughed.

I thought maybe we would wait until the next week or the next month. They were at my house the next day! I thought he was going to drop the kids off and leave. He stayed!

Will and his children were entertaining themselves with Connect Four that belonged to my girls. I was in my kitchen cooking. My back was to the entrance.

"Smells good in here," he said.

I could not turn around. I was stuck. *For some odd reason, the tone of his voice sent chills down my spine and caused my heart to skip some beats.*

"It is going to taste delicious," I said, slowly turning around.

"My kids will be the judge of that," he laughed.

"Oh! They are going to love it!" I laughed.

I was exactly right! His kids loved my homemade chicken and dumplings. My kitchen table had empty bowls sitting on it as the kids got up from the table to head back into my living room. I began to clean the table. He went to my living room to turn a movie on for them. He then came back into the kitchen and helped me clear the table.

"From the looks of their bowl and your bowl, my chicken and dumplings were delicious."

He laughed, "Yeah, they were"

"Aww!" I laughed, "Thank you! Was that hard?"

"Very!" he laughed.

"So, I cook better than you?" I asked him.

He laughed, "I am not answering that."

We both began to wash the dishes. I cleaned as he dried.

"I mean, there are somethings that I expect women to do better than me," he said, "I am not afraid to admit that."

"Explain," I said.

"Cook, clean, wash and fold clothes! I hate

folding the kid's clothes. How do y'all do it?"

I laughed and said, "It's easy!"

"You can have it."

"About cleaning. You think women are supposed to clean. Your house must be filthy."

Will laughed. "You got jokes! Naw! My house is clean. I'm just saying. You would probably clean up better than me. I may miss a spot."

"Yeah, yeah! If you're a nineteenth-century man, just say that."

Will laughed. "Nowhere near it. Women are capable like men, but I do believe there are some things you all are made to do."

I turned and looked at him so fast. He laughed.

"Let me finish, woman!"

I rolled my eyes. He snatched a spoon out of my hand to dry it with the towel.

"I do believe there are some things women are made to do better than a man."

"Nice, finish!" I laughed.

"Whatever, woman!"

He put the last bowl into my dry rack. We dried our hands and made our way to my back patio. I sat down in one chair. He sat in the other.

"When are you coming back to church?" he asked me.

I sighed and looked up into the night sky.

"How did you know I attended Temple of Heaven?" I asked.

He then said, "I guessed you attended when

you suggested it to me, but I never see you there. I see all your friends when I go."

"I will go back one day," I said to him.

"Why did you stop?" he asked me.

I was silent. I was not ready yet to share that information with him.

"When you do not want to talk, you get quiet," he said.

He was right, and I was not ready to tell him either. So, I kept quiet.

"When you like something or when you're excited about something, you turn into the ultimate queen of comedy," he said.

Now I had to laugh at him. I looked at him and rolled my eyes.

"Those eyes get to rolling when you don't want to agree with someone," he smiled.

I rolled my eyes again. He was right. I did not want to agree with him. He laughed! I looked back out into my backyard. He was paying attention to me. Why was it making me feel some type of way? I mean, I wasn't upset about it, but I wasn't crazy, either. The man was starting to worry about me and pay attention to me. Something was going on with his feelings.

"Yesterday was a good day, and this evening what nice. I hope dinner at Italian Bistro tomorrow will be nice."

I slowly looked at him. He smiled. I squinted at him. He winked at me. I laughed and rolled my eyes.

"You already brought me lunch from there."

"But I have not eaten there," he said to me.

Italian Bistro was not a restaurant that you showed up to without a reservation. I had to test him to see if we were really going there.

"What time is the reservation?" I asked him.

Will smiled. "Eight-thirty. We're going after the group session."

I laughed and looked away. He actually made reservations. He was serious about going out. I accepted the invitation.

Will

I was late for the group session. Junior was fighting at school. By the time I arrived, the facilitator was separating the group into individual groups. I sat down at the table with Kim. She smiled but then lost the smile. I knew she could tell I was upset.

"What happened?" she asked me.

I really needed to get things off my chest. I went right into it,

"Junior was fighting at school today. Apparently, some kids were bullying Ryleigh. I am okay with him standing up for his sister. I am upset about the level of anger he used when fighting. If he had been an adult, he would have been charged! It was bad!"

"Well, maybe you can talk to him about it later when you get home," she suggested, "Hear him out and then use his reasoning to help you help him. Also, let him know the different ways to take up for his sister."

Her suggestions were great. I was so caught up in my mess that I did not realize she was talking in the group session.

"You're talking!" I blurted out.

Everyone in the room turned our way. She quickly turned toward me. She eyed me, folded her arms, and threw herself back into the chair. I knew she was about to stop talking.

"I am sorry!" I said. I then began to plead, "Do not stop talking!"

"Gotcha!" she said, laughing.

Everyone in the room laughed. I took a piece of paper from my binder, balled it up, and threw it at her. She kept on laughing.

The group session ended at 7:00 p.m. Our reservation for Italian Bistro was at 8:30 p.m. We had a little time in between time. She told me she would meet me there. I decided to go home and have that talk with my son.

The talk with Junior was not bad at all. I did use what Kim suggested. I understood my son. My son understood other alternatives, such as letting me know, informing teachers or staff, and encouraging his sister. I felt good after the talk. I felt good enough to put on a little something for dinner. I chose my black slacks with the dark red dress shirt and the red bow tie. Ryleigh peeped her head into my room as I straightened the bow tie.

"GG is here," she said. My mother moved to Crestview with me to help me take care of my children.

"That means you are going out," she said, folding her arms.

I laughed and said, "I am going out."

"With who?" she snapped.

I slowly turned to her. Before I almost tore into her behind, I asked her to come to me. She rushed over to me and fell into my arms. She began to cry. I sat her in my lap on the bed.

"I want you to stay with me," she cried.

I couldn't discipline my baby. I needed to hear her out.

"I am always with you. I will never leave you," I said to her.

"We used to do stuff with Mama like we do with Dr. Kim, and then you left us," she cried.

I then knew why my daughter was crying. Ryleigh was afraid I would leave her if I got too close to Kim. My daughter did have memories of the constant arguing and fighting with her mom. After the arguments, we were right back to family dinners and outings before we divorced. I did leave my children with her believing we could co-parent, and their life was turned completely upside down.

"That is not going to happen," I said to her.

"I do like Dr. Kim," said Ryleigh, "I just don't want you to leave."

"I am not leaving you or your brother ever again."

"Okay. Are you going to see Dr. Kim?"

"I am," I laughed.

"Okay," smiled Ryleigh. "Tell her I said hi Tell her not to take you away from us."

I squeezed my baby girl tight. "Dr. Kim likes you and your brother. She is going to take me away from you."

"Okay," said Ryleigh. "Still tell her what I said."

"I gotcha, big girl!" I smiled.

Ryleigh looked up at me. She then looked down at my dress shirt, slacks, and shoes. I chuckled. She was checking her father out.

"Do I look nice?" I asked her.

She nodded her head. I kissed my baby on her cheek.

"Thank you. You have fun with GiGi and your brother tonight, okay? Don't think about Daddy leaving you. I am coming back to you."

"Yes, sir. Okay," she smiled.

I stood up from the bed with my girl in my arms. She wasn't too big for her daddy to carry. I walked her downstairs to the kitchen with my mother and junior. The two of them were rolling cookie dough.

"Look what you were missing," I said to Ryleigh.

She was ready to get down once she saw the cookie dough. My girl loved sweets. My mother turned around. She checked me out too. From head to toe.

"You're dressed up for Dr. Kim," she smiled.

"Italian Bistro is not a casual restaurant," I said, leaning against the kitchen counter.

"And I'm your father!" laughed my mother. "Son, I know you. You got dressed up for Dr. Kim. Come talk to me."

We left the kids at the kitchen table, rolling cooking dough. We both sat down on the couch in my living room.

"What's going on with you and Dr. Kim?"

"This is going to sound bad," I said to my mother.

My mother folded her arms. She tilted her head to the side, waiting for my explanation.

"She's my support partner for the group. Except she doesn't talk during the group session. I went digging for some information. I found out she likes chocolate ice cream. The other night when I asked you to come over, I invited her out. The conversation was actually good. I told her to let me know when she got home. Again, I'm her support partner. Well, when she called. I didn't want to get off the phone with her. We got to know each other a little more. Your grandkids came in the room, and it led to us going over to her house for chicken and dumplings. I got to know her some more."

My mother nodded her head. "Okay, so let me get this straight, you're attracted to your kids' doctor, which is also your support partner."

I didn't want to tell my mother she was right. I laughed and said, "I get two versions of her. I'll just say that I like the happy and fun Kim."

My mother laughed. "You're attracted to the happy and fun Kim who you are getting to know."

"Plus, she's a pretty brown skin, like somebody else I know."

My mother smiled. "Like your mother."

I smiled. "The first woman I loved."

"I love you too, Son."

My mother hugged me. She rubbed my back. "Be careful. She's your support partner and the kid's doctor. You are crossing boundaries. I trust you, though."

"I've thought about those," I smiled, standing up from the couch.

"You're grown," smiled Mama. "I just thought to remind you."

"Thank you, Mama."

"You're welcome. Enjoy yourself."

I gave my mama another hug before leaving. I arrived right on time for our reservation. Kim hadn't made it yet. I was busy on my phone. I did not see her come up to the table or walk up to the table.

"Hey," she said.

Her figure in the all-black fitted mini dress had my eyes glued. If I wanted to look away, I couldn't! Kim wasn't a slim or plus-size woman. The dress showed me just how thick she was. The dress covered her breast. I saw enough to make me want to see more. My eyes traveled down her body to her silver heels and back up to the matching bracelet and earrings. I liked her dressed up. I was so used to seeing her in the white coat and scrubs or the normal hoodie and sweatpants. Her hair was different. Normally it was in a natural ponytail pulled back. Her natural curls hung to her shoulders. Did she have on make-up? Yes! She did! Her red lips were very appealing. They made me want to lick mine! The natural eye shadow made me stare into her eyes. Her dark brown eyes almost hypnotized me.

Kim

The man was staring at me! I knew I should have left the dress in the closet! He did not even speak back! I wanted to throw the entire outfit away! I decided to play with him.

"When I count to seven, you shall be in heaven...."

He had the nerve to play along,

"You can start counting!" he winked.

Yeah, he was showing out! I laughed as he got up from his seat. He pulled my chair out for me. I sat down.

"You look nice," he said to me.

His eyes said that already. I wanted to say that, but I thanked him instead. He picked up the menu looking at the selections. I already knew what I was going to order.

"Since this is your favorite restaurant, what are your top selections?"

He asked me a hard question. Italian Bistro's entire menu was good. I took a minute to think.

"I love Italian food anyway. I would have to go with the three-meat lasagna for third place. The second place would be the pepper platter. My number one choice is their version of □."

"Baked penne pasta," he said, finishing my sentence.

I smiled. He was right.

"That is what I ordered for you when I sent you lunch."

I was still trying to figure out how he knew so much about me.

"You did," I smiled. "I'm not ordering that tonight. The whole menu is delicious. I'm going to order the alfredo zucchini boats."

"Well, since you're not ordering your favorite, I'll order it. I want to try it out."

"You'll like it!" I smiled. "It's your choice of meatballs or chicken topped with more cheese and pasta sauce. Oh my God! It's so good!"

The waitress came to take our drink orders. We were ready to order. Will let me place my order first, and then he gave his order. We were sitting and waiting for the waitress to come back with our drinks.

"Tell me about the journey to being Dr. Kim."

I laughed. "Um, my maternal great great grandfather was the first physician here in Crestview."

"That's what's up! You have a huge legacy here."

"I do," I smiled. "My great-grandfather was a doctor. His daughter, my grandmother, was a doctor. My mom is a nurse practitioner. I chose to follow my grandmother's footsteps and become a pediatrician."

"Wow! Never would have known that!"

"You seem to know everything about me! I don't know why you didn't find that out!"

"My source didn't say that," he laughed.

I had to ask what made him want to become an engineering manager.

The waitress bringing our drinks back to the table interrupted him. "Thank you," he said to her as she placed an Arnold Palmer in front of him. She placed an iced tea in front of me. She took our orders, walked away, and he continued.

"We have a lot in common," said Will. "My family history influenced my career choice as well. My grandfather and father both are retired engineers. I started out as an engineer. I work with Rowan HVAC."

"I didn't know Rowan had an HVAC site."

"Yeah, we supply the local companies and stores in Crestview, Rowan, Grunsville, and Tillmore with systems. We have some out-of-state buyers. I come up with plans for new systems. I have to create budgets, order equipment, supervise my team of engineers, and work with other managers. Besides spades, what else do you like to play?"

I laughed. I did love me some spades. "I'll play a game of gin rummy."

"You'll have to teach me how to play that."

"Really!"

"Yes!" he laughed.

"You are a good spades, partner. What are

some things you like to do when you're not working or busy with your kids?"

"I like to travel to different locations. It doesn't matter how big or small. I like to see the scenery. If there are things to do, that's fine. If not, I'm content."

"Scenic traveling, interesting."

"Do you like to travel?"

"I do," I said. "I haven't been anywhere lately. Not with everything going on with my girls."

"I understand. Same here," he said. "I have been focused on my kids."

We were quiet for a minute. I don't think either one of us wanted to get on the subject of our children and their issues. Will started a new conversation.

"I want to know more about how you feel about gender roles."

I decided to hit him with, "I was a wife. Who married under traditional vows."

He was quiet. He nodded his head. He came back with, "I was a husband who married under traditional vows."

"I guess we are on the same page," I smiled.

The waitress came back to the table with our entrees. We skipped appetizers. The zucchini boats were on point, as I knew they would be. Will was enjoying the baked penne pasta.

"This is very good," he said, wiping his mouth with a napkin.

"I told you so," I smiled.

He looked over at my food. "Can you cut a piece, and I'll get it with my fork, or would you rather feed it to me?"

I was in the middle of drinking my iced tea. I almost spit it across the table. He thought it was funny. I swallowed the tea with a laugh.

"I'm the wrong person to play with!"

"If you're scared to feed me in public, I understand."

I rolled my eyes at him. I cut a piece of the zucchini boat. He had his fork ready. I snatched it from him. He laughed at me. I stuck the fork in the zucchini.

"Open wide little William!" I said.

He laughed while opening his mouth. I fed the zucchini to him. I watched him chew. He wiped his mouth with a nod.

"Man! That's good too!"

"Yep! They don't hit and miss here! They hit every time!"

"One thing," he said.

"What's that?"

"It's big, Will, to you."

I laughed so hard! I wasn't expecting him to come back like that! I blushed for a second.

He ate the last of the pasta. He asked me if I had any plans for the remainder of the evening. I wanted to say duh! I needed to go home and get some rest! I had to be at work the next morning! He was acting like it was the weekend! My schedule was full the following day. My mouth hurried and said,

"No."

Look at the lies! *I should have told him the truth. What was going on with me?*

"I have been looking around Crestview. There are a few spots I want to visit. I know you don't want to go because you feel people gossip," he said.

"You are right!" I said. "I don't need anybody saying we are together."

Will eyed me. "I wouldn't want them to say we are together either. Not yet, anyway."

"Not yet," I repeated.

Will laughed. He looked away for a second. He lowered his head and looked back up at me.

"Kim, we aren't at dinner by mistake. There is something clearly going on here. I'm just telling you the truth. I want to check out the spots with you. I want to learn more about you. I think we are friends. Suppose our friendship leads to dating and then a relationship. Okay, I'm ready for that."

His truth had my heart beating fast. I knew something was going on between us. I didn't want to accept it. I had so much going on.

"I respect you for giving it to me straight," I said. I cleared my throat. I took a deep breath and let it out.

"Will, I know something is going on too. I tried to ignore it. At the same time, I can't ignore the issues in my life right now."

Will nodded his head. "I understand. We both have a lot going on. You know about my children.

You don't know everything. I don't expect you to tell me everything about your girls. I hope that we both can work on that."

"I don't know about anything," I said honestly. "I can't give you an answer."

"That's fine," he smiled. "I have no problem with pursuing you."

I laughed. "I think you have already started."

He smiled. "So, since you know, keep going with the flow. I don't need you to do anything else."

He had me smiling. "I'm your kids' doctor."

"Yeah, I'm attracted to their doctor!"

I had to laugh at him. He laughed as well.

"Look, I'm not changing their doctor. I guess we will have to learn to keep it professional at the office."

"I would appreciate that," I smiled.

"I got you, Doc. No worries. Jewels is one of your favorite places. How about we leave your favorite restaurant and head to your favorite lounge?

I was quiet. There he was again, telling me something he knew about me. I could not seem to figure out where he was getting the information.

"You like to dance..." he said, adding to the list of things about me.

I was still quiet. He knew the drill. He smiled and said,

"You can drop your car off at your place, and you can ride with me."

Lord, why did I find myself parking my car in

my driveway? Lord, why was I getting in his car? Lord, why was he so excited? Lord, why was he pulling into the parking lot of Jewels? Lord, why did I get out and go inside? My nerves were terrible! I needed a drink. I could get wine. Jesus turned water into wine! I stopped at the bar and ordered a bottle of wine! Why did he tell the bartender to start a tab? On him! He was paying! I was letting him pay!

We were sitting at the table. He had not drunk any of the wine! It was down to the bottom! Almost gone! I poured another glass. He laughed,

"You, okay?"

"Huh, uh," I mumbled as I swallowed the wine.

"Let's dance," he said.

That was my cue to finish the bottle of wine! I grabbed the bottle and poured the rest. He laughed and shook his head.

"Calm down," he said, taking the bottle from me. "Give me the glass?"

Lord! I gave him the glass of wine! He somehow managed to take my hand in the process. Lord, why were his hands soothing? The next thing I knew, he was gently pulling me from my seat, and I was following him to the dance floor—the sounds of "If This World Were Mine" by Luther Vandross hit my ears. I was not ready!

We stopped in the middle of the floor. Other people were there, but I felt we were the only ones on the floor. I almost melted when he gently placed his arms around my waist. That was my cue to place mine around his neck or at least rest them on his shoulders! I could not! Before I knew it, this man had done it for me!

Our bodies moved from left to right. I eased my right hand down his chest before resting it there. I looked up, and our eyes locked. I gave him a soft smile. He leaned his head down closer. I prepared myself for his lips to touch mine. Instead, his nose found mine. He probably felt how tense I was and decided not to go with the kiss. I relaxed my body, and he pulled me closer.

Will

One thing I liked about Crestview was that most businesses were black-owned. I was ready to try the candy store with Kim. She had been there before. She mentioned that the owner always makes new candy for the residents to try.

I swooped her up from her place. I pulled into the empty parking lot. The white sign on the small red brick building read, "Shandra's Sweets and Treats," in pink letters. Kim was shocked to see that the parking lot was empty.

"This is strange! When there is new candy, this place is packed!"

"She's been advertising it for weeks," I said.

"Right!" said Kim. "Is she open?"

We got out of the Camaro and headed to the door. The store was open. I pulled the door open for Kim. She walked inside.

"Hey Kim," said the owner, coming from the back of the shop.

"Hey, Shandra! Girl, where are the people?"

"No people today! We have a special tasting today."

"Huh?" asked Kim.

Shandra looked at me with a smile. Kim

turned around to me.

"What did you do?"

"I'll tell you in a minute," I said. "Shandra, show us the way."

"Right this way," said Shandra, leading us to the back of the candy store.

Shandra went into a small room. Kim followed her. She stopped at the entrance of the door.

"Aww! Y'all!"

She turned and looked at me. "Will! You get on my nerves! Everything is nice!"

I walked up, standing behind her. The setup of the room was nice. I hadn't seen it. I only told Shandra what I wanted. She did a great job. The entire room was decorated in Kim's favorite color, yellow. A yellow tablecloth covered the table in the middle of the room. Yellow roses and daisies sat on the table in a clear yellow vase. In the corner was a small table with another yellow tablecloth and chocolate on a yellow dish. There was a draped white and yellow backdrop on the far wall.

"Enjoy," said Shandra, leaving us in the room.

I took Kim by her hand, leading her over to the chocolate. I picked up a piece with a yellow napkin. I held it up to her mouth. She tasted the candy.

"Yes! That is good."

"I'm glad you like it. This is the new chocolate she made. I scheduled this private tasting for us to enjoy ourselves. I know you want us to keep things

THE RECIPE OF A GODLY WOMAN IV

private. If I'm honest, I had to go home and really think about what you said. I understand why now. You do have a lot going on in your life. I'm not trying to add to it. I don't want you worried when you should be having a good time."

Her eyes glazed over as she looked into mine. I didn't want her to cry. I wanted her to know how much I respected her feelings. I hated to interrupt the sentimental moment, but I didn't want her to cry. I hurried and took her over to the backdrop.

"You like to take pictures, take out that phone, and let's get this over with!"

Kim laughed and took out her phone. I stood behind her while she snapped a selfie of us. I planted a kiss on her cheek. She snapped another selfie.

I wasn't a picture kind of guy. I let Kim take as many pictures as she wanted. When she was done turning all kinds of ways for angles, I made her sit at the table. I brought the chocolate over to the table for her. She didn't get a chance to feed herself at all. I fed her every piece of candy.

"This was very thoughtful of you," she said to me. "I don't want you to start doing private things with me or for me. It would be a lot."

"It's not a problem," I said to her.

"I understand that. It's also not fair to you. You shouldn't have to hide your choice of who you are choosing to date because of my past or because of the people here in Crestview."

"I don't want you stressed," I said.

Kim smirked. "No matter what is going on in your life in Crestview. If people want to talk, they are going to talk. They will talk about the good and the bad. They seem to stretch the bad things out and make them seem worse."

I was willing to keep things private to protect Kim. I didn't know the people in Crestview. I didn't care about what they said about me. Those folks didn't know me.

"Are you sure?" I asked her.

"I'm sure," she said.

I rubbed my finger down the left side of her face. She took my hand and rested her face in the palm of my hand. Her eyes met mine, and she smiled. I inhaled and exhaled.

Will

I knew how to bowl. I hadn't been in a minute. Some of the guys at work were talking about going with their wives. They invited me even though I was not married. The bowling alley was one of the places I had been thinking about giving a try. There was no way I could show up without a date. I called Kim to see if she would come with me. I laughed when she told me,

"Um yeah, cause who else are you going with?"

We walked into the bowling alley together. The crowd was decent. We walked over to the counter to get shoes. She took a size eight. I ordered a size thirteen. I grabbed her shoes from the counter for her. I spotted my team of engineers at lane ten. We headed over to the group. I introduced her to everyone. She seemed to be okay with being out in public with me. Once we got our shoes on, it was time for us to start the game with the rest of the crew. One of the guys suggested we team up with our significant others. Whichever team had the most points would win. Kim face palmed herself.

"What?" I asked her.

"I don't know how to bowl!"

I laughed. "It's okay. I don't lose with anybody but you."

"Lose!" she said. "Mane! We ain't losing. You finna teach me real quick!"

"Okay, okay," I laughed. "I'm going to get you a ball."

Since this was her first-time bowling, I chose a light ball for her. A size ten was best. When I returned to the table, I saw her watching everyone else bowl.

"This is your ball," I said, showing her the yellow ball I picked out for her.

"Oh! It's yellow!" she said. "Yeah, we finna win!"

"Alright," I laughed, taking the ball to the rack.

I was nervous when it was my turn to bowl. I knew Kim was watching me. I picked up my red ball from the rack. I held the ball in my hand. I prepared myself to bowl. I released the ball. It went down the lane full speed hitting the pins. All the pins fell! Strike! I turned around to see Kim smiling and clapping for me. We high-fived. It was her turn. I handed her the yellow ball.

"I want to put my fingers in it."

"What? I can't have you breaking your fingers!"

Kim laughed. "Shut up! I'm not breaking my fingers! Show me how."

I showed her how to place her fingers in the

ball. She walked up to the line, ready to throw the ball down the lane.

"Wait," I said, standing behind her. I held her wrist, maneuvering it so she could release the ball.

"I got it," she said.

She let the ball go. It was going at a pretty good speed. She leaned back into me, watching it go down the lane. I wrapped my arms around her waist. The ball hit the pins, and they all fell! She jumped into my arms.

"I got a strike!"

"You did!"

I heard an engineer on my team say, "Naw! Look at y'all cheating! You can't go back up there with her!"

Kim laughed while I carried her back to my seat. I sat down with her in my lap. I looked up at the scores on the mounted screen. We were in the lead.

Kim

Every week, Thursday was a walk-in day at the clinic. It was our busiest day of the week. We barely had lunch. Will knew how busy we were on Wednesdays. I mentioned it to him. I barely had time to talk to him on Thursdays. Mainly because I was tired after work, I would go home and go right to sleep.

On Thursdays, my staff took a thirty-minute lunch break instead of an hour. I was standing at the receptionist's desk, turning in a file. My nurse practitioner was on her way out of the front door for lunch. A delivery man was on his way in with a box. He was from the Crestview Deli.

"Who ordered lunch?" I asked.

"We didn't," said my receptionist.

My nurse practitioner, receptionists, and three nurses were just as confused as I was. The delivery man sat the box down on the counter.

"This is for Kim and her staff from Will."

My cell then began to vibrate in my white coat pocket. I took it out to see Will calling.

"Hello," I said.

"Did you get the lunch?" he asked.

"We did, thank you so much. You're too sweet."

"You're welcome. Lunch will be there every Thursday."

"No, they won't. You don't have to do that."

"Yes, they will, and don't tell me what to do, woman. Go ahead and eat. I know y'all only have a little time left. Stop by the house when you get off. I don't want to hear anything about it being late, either. Cause I'll come get you from your house!"

"Alright!" I laughed. "Thank you again! I will see you later."

I was late getting off. Charting from a Thursday could not go into a Friday. We would never get done. It was eight thirty when I made it to Will's house. I stood outside his house, knocking on the door. He opened his front door, trying to act like he was mad.

"Now, why didn't you tell me you were on the way? I could have the door open for you."

"Look," I said, walking into his house. "I have typed so many charts. I could not lift my fingers to call you."

"I'mma let you slide this time," he said. "The kids are with my mom tonight. Head upstairs to the room. I'll be there in a minute."

I was glad he didn't have a lot of stairs. Once I reached the top of the stairs, I was happy his room was right by the staircase. I turned the corner, and a smile immediately came across my face. This man had a black silk robe on the bed. I picked it up and headed for the bathroom. I opened the bathroom door to see a hot bubble bath waiting for me. I smiled at the roses floating on top of the bubbles. I undressed, stepping into the hot water. The water soothed me as I slid down under the bubbles. I relaxed, leaning my head back against the tub.

"I see you found the bubble bath," said Will.

I opened my eyes to see him standing in the

bathroom doorway.

"Thank you," I said.

He smiled at me. "When was the last time you had a day to yourself? I'm not talking about hiding in your house, in the bed, under the covers. I'm talking about a day where you rested."

I sighed. "What are you trying to say?"

"I'm saying you don't take off. I know you are driving to see Mya. You won't tell me about Mia. I'm still not pressing it. I know your daughters are always on your mind. We have our group session. I think you need a day to yourself."

"Who is this talking to me?" I asked him. "Are you being my support partner, or are you being Will the pursuer?"

Will leaned against his bathroom wall. "I'm being a man who is starting to care about a woman by the second. I'm being the man for the woman I see myself with in the future. I'm going to pay attention to you. I will let you know what I feel is best for you."

I lowered my head. I was listening and taking in what he was saying to me. Small pieces of my heart were starting to soften up for him.

Will smiled at me. "Get ya mind right now. I'll be taking care of you."

I laughed. "Whatever, Will!"

He laughed. He walked to the tub, kneeled, and pushed my natural curls back. He ran his hand down the right side of my face.

"I want you to stay here tonight. You know the kind of man I am. I don't want anything from you. At least not yet," he laughed.

I rolled my eyes at him. "Boy, you gon' need more than group therapy after you get this."

Will bit his bottom lip. "Sign me up for the

services, doc."

I laughed. I stared at him. I wanted to hand him over the reigns. I was still afraid. I closed my eyes and took a deep breath.

"What else are you trying to say, Will?"

He smiled at me. "This is the Kim I like. I think you should take tomorrow off. You need a day. It's okay to have a day to rest and reboot."

I had to throw him bait. I wanted to see where his mind was.

"You must be taking off tomorrow?"

"No," he said. "I'm going to work."

"What? I may as well go home. You're not going to be here."

Will shook his head. "No. Dinner is waiting on us in the kitchen. Call whoever you need to call at the clinic about tomorrow. My arms are ready to hold you all night. Breakfast will be ready for you in the morning. A key will be on the kitchen counter if you feel like leaving. My card will be with the key if you're not gone by noon. Order your lunch. Any questions?"

I smiled at him. "No, Sir."

"Alright, I'll be in the kitchen when you're ready for dinner," he said, getting up from the side of the tub. I couldn't help but watch that man walk out of the bathroom. He was doing something to me.

Audrey

Lunch with my friends happened at least once a week. It was my turn to pick the restaurant. I chose Seafood Galore! The best seafood restaurant in the city. It was new and popular. We arrived on time for our reservation. Allison, Lauren, and I were seated at a table. Kim had not arrived. We just knew she was going to stand us up. Since her daughters had been away, she had not been herself. Allison was about to call her when Lauren asked,

"Is that Kim walking in the door?"

I was a bit shocked! To my surprise, it was her! I was shocked because she was not wearing scrubs! She was, in fact, in a fitted red dress with heels. She wore make-up! I mean, her face was beat! Her hair was out of the regular ponytail. She didn't even have her natural curls. Her silk press was flawless in the asymmetrical bob.

"No!" said Allison, "Must be someone else."

I laughed and eyed Allison, "That is her!"

Kim approached the table, "Hey ladies!"

We all were silent. Lauren started at her feet and made her way up her body to her hair.

"Who are you, and where is Kim?" she asked.

"You are not funny!" said Kim dropping down into the seat.

Allison smirked, "Someone is really happy, I see."

"I just decided to put clothes on!" snapped Kim.

"Make-up and heels, too!" said Allison, "Your hair is cute!"

"Who did you let do yo hair? You didn't come to the shop! They didn't do a better job than me!" snapped Lauren, "What's going on?

Kim laughed at Lauren. "I'm sorry, boo!" She picked up the menu, "I just feel better."

After lunch, I headed back to the clinic. Allison tagged along. Allison was sitting at my desk, flipping through a magazine. I reviewed the x-rays of a dog hit by a car.

"I do not know how to approach something," she said.

I slowly looked up at her. I leaned back in my chair.

"I'm listening," I said.

"You know I see and hear everything!"

I cut her off, "You know how I feel about gossip!"

"Thing is, it is about my best friend."

I sighed and said, "We were just with Kim! We all were together! Why did you not ask then?"

Allison said, "Well, because we were in the restaurant."

"I do not want to hear any gossip or lies!

What are you trying to approach her about?"

"Well, I've heard Will ordered her lunch one day. She was at the west side café late one night with Will. They have been at one another's house! They were out for dinner at Italian Bistro and even seen hugged up at Jewel's! They have been all over Crestview together."

I threw the x-rays on my desk and folded my arms, "I asked you not to give me gossip!"

"Well, don't respond to it!" said Allison, "You won't be gossiping then, first lady! You just listened."

"So, just ask her if she is dating Will," I said.
"It is obvious that something is going on," said Allison, "She was all dolled up today!"

I sighed, "Why can't you just ask her?"

"I can't ask her because Will has been with someone else in the town! If I ask her, I will have to tell her that. I don't know if that is true either!"

I placed my hand over my face, "I'm done talking about this."

Allison threw the magazine onto my desk. I shook my head at her and went back to looking at the x-rays.

Will

Every Sunday after church, I had dinner with the children. I decided to invite Kim. I gave her a ring. She answered on the first ring.

"Hey," she said.

The way she said, "hey," had ya boy smiling.

"Hey, what you doing? You busy?"

"No," she said. "What's up?"

"I'm having Sunday dinner with the kids if you want to come."

"Sure," she said.

"I'm coming to get you," I said to her.

"Oh! Okay," she said. "What time?"

"Will you be ready in an hour?"

"I can be. Wait, is this a formal dinner or what?"

I laughed. "Just dress comfortably."

"Alrighty," said Kim. "See you in a minute."

"See you later," I said.

I gave her an hour with an extra five minutes. I pulled my Yukon Denali into her driveway. I was about to give her a ring when I saw the front door opening. She must have been waiting for me. That made a brotha feel good. I told her to dress comfortably. She hadn't been wearing the jeans and hoodie lately. I thought I was going to see the outfit. Instead, she wore a loose lavender dress with a jean jacket. The dress still didn't hide those thick hips of hers. I smiled at the sight of her as I got out. I walked over to the passenger side. We hugged before I opened the door for her. She got in, and I closed the door, walked back to the driver's side, hopped back into the seat, and were on our way.

She looked in the empty backseat. "Where are Junior and Ryleigh?"

"Already there," I said.

"You left them at home alone?"

"What?" I laughed. "No!"

"Audrey or somebody is with them?"

"No," I said.

"Well, where are they?"

"Just ride," I laughed.

Kim eyed me. "Where are we going?"

"Why can't you just ride?"

"You said we were having dinner with the kids. They are not here. You said they are already there. If our friends are not with them, they are somewhere where our friends are not. Again, where are we going?"

"Ride with me, okay? We are going to the kids."

"You're up to something," laughed Kim.

"Of course I am," I laughed. "For now, sit back and relax."

We entered a neighborhood. Kim read the

sign.

"Addison Crossing. I don't know anybody who lives in this neighborhood."

"I know somebody," I laughed.

"Clearly," laughed Kim.

We drove for another three blocks. I turned into an empty driveway. I put the truck in park and shut off the engine. Kim quickly turned to me. "We are here now! Whose house is this?"

I laughed and got out of the car. I walked over to the passenger side. I opened the door for her. I reached out for her hand. She took my hand. I helped her down. I closed the door behind her. I led her to the door. I used my key to open the door. She froze.

"You have a key!"

"Yes," I laughed.

"Whose house is this?"

"Look, woman," I laughed. "Go inside."

Kim walked through the front door of the house. I could smell the fried chicken.

"Who is cooking?" she asked me.

I knew she would smell the food. I smiled. I didn't say a word. I took her by her hand again. We walked down the hallway that led to the backyard. I pulled the patio back. We walked outside to see Ryleigh swinging on the swings. Junior was riding his bike.

"Dr. Kim!" said Ryleigh hopping off the swings.

Junior stopped his bike. He got off so fast

when he saw Kim.

"Hey, y'all!" she said, accepting their hugs.

"Watch me swing!" said Ryleigh.

"Watch me on my bike!" said Junior. "I am going to go fast!"

"Alright! Let me see," she smiled.

Ryleigh took back off to the swings. Junior ran back to his bike.

"So, you have two houses?" she asked without taking her eyes off my kids.

"Yep! This one is in my name too!" I said.

She turned her attention to me. "What?"

"Nothing," I said.

Scratching on the patio door caught both of our attention. We turned around to see two tan and black Yorkies. One was scratching on the door.

"Harlo! I told you about scratching on the door," I said to the dog wearing the green collar. Both dogs ran outside when I opened the door. Harlo took off to the kids. Haskel, with the yellow collar, stayed.

"Oh my goodness!" said Kim. "Hey!"

She picked up Haskel. She looked at me, "You don't have dogs at your house! What is going on?"

I smiled, ignored her, and watched her play with Haskel. Kim walked to a chair at a small table and sat down. I followed her and sat across from her. I couldn't help but stare at her. I liked to see her happy. She noticed I was staring.

"What?" she asked me.

"Nothing, Baby. You're just beautiful."

Kim

I could have dropped the dog! I almost squeezed it to death! Poor thing! I tried to find the "thank you," but it would not come out. The man called me baby. Since when did we go from real names to pet names?

"I have enjoyed spending time with you," he said, "I have enjoyed it so much that I want to get a little closer to you."

I was choking the dog by then. My heart was beating fast too. It was time to put the poor dog down. I did just that, and it ran off. Poor baby was scared!

He moved his chair closer to me, "You're silent."

I lowered my head and said, "Will, we have talked about this. My issues are still here."

"We both have issues," he said. "I have children who are suffering from mental and behavioral health issues. You won't tell me what is going on with your daughters. I'm not pressuring you, either. I know you were once married. I feel your previous relationship has something to do with your resistance to me."

"Will, I have so much going on. I do not think

I will be what you need me to be."

"What happened to you going with the flow?"

I sighed. "When I go with the flow…."

I had to stop myself. I couldn't let him know everything. I lowered my head. I heard Will say,

"When you go with the flow, you're not in control. You don't want to give me too much power."

I looked up at him. He was right. I couldn't roll my eyes because they glossed over with tears I was fighting to hold back.

"We don't have to talk about it right now. I didn't plan on talking about it here," he said. "I brought you here today to show you how much you mean to me. I do want to move forward with you. I want to work toward a relationship. I want to keep sending you flowers, I want to constantly wine and dine with you, and I want us to have more date nights. I want to grow to family outings eventually. I want to grow with you, Kim. What do you say to us moving forward?"

The man was fine! I was not going to say yes just because he was dark chocolate fine! My heart was working on parting my lips to say yes. I was attracted to the tall, dark, handsome, and muscular man. He was bringing me back to life! He was helping me live again. I was afraid that I would stop living again. Not because of him but because there was so much going on in my life. I was not ready for another relationship. I was willing to try it even though I was not ready. I was about to answer when an older woman opened the patio door and stepped outside. Her salt and pepper curled hair and dark complexion told me she was his mother.

"Hello," she said, smiling at me. She walked over to the table. "You must be Kim!"

I stood up and hugged her, "Hello! Yes, I am."

"I am Rose," she said, smiling as she admired me from head to toe.

Meanwhile, I was about to pass out! I made eye contact with Will to save me. He stood up, standing behind me. He slid his left arm around my back, slightly pulling me to him. His touch eased my nerves.

"Nice to meet you," I smiled.

"It's good to meet you finally," she smiled.

She looked up at Will. "You snuck her in on me!"

I looked up at him. "Oh, so you're surprising everyone today."

"I did," he smiled.

His mother smiled at me. "What are we going to do with him?"

"I have no idea!" I laughed.

"You two head on in. The food is ready on the table. I'm going to get the kids cleaned up," she said.

His mother prepared dinner. It was just like when I was a little girl. Homemade collard greens, macaroni cheese, mashed potatoes, fried chicken, and rolls. I was ready to get the recipe for her homemade lemonade. The food was better than delicious. More like scrumptious!

Ms. Rose was a very sweet lady. She and I talked over dinner. We joked and laughed. I enjoyed my time at her house. I even helped her clear the table and wash the dishes. I was putting the last glass in her cabinet when she said,

"I look forward to more Sundays with you."

"Same here," I smiled.

After we finished the dishes, she was still in the kitchen, straightening up things. I walked out of the kitchen and felt Will grabbing my body. He pulled me to him. He kissed me, and my body went limp. My knees buckled. He held me tight to keep me from falling. Kim said, "pull away," but Kimberly said, "Girl, kiss that man back." I eased up, wrapped my arms around his neck, and gently pressed my lips against his. Our tongues met one another for the first time. I felt his hands ease down my back. We unlocked our lips, and he said,

"I heard what you said to my mama."

I smiled and rolled my eyes. Will laughed and kissed me on the cheek.

The kids wanted to spend the night with their grandma. Will let them stay. I gave them hugs and kisses before leaving. While Will drove me back to my house, I looked out of the window at the night sky.

"I met your mother today," I said, looking back on the day.

"You did," he said. "I'm serious about us, Kim."

"I see," I said.

Will taking me to meet his mother was major. If he wanted to be with me, he would accept everything that came with me. I felt that, but I needed assurance.

He pulled into my driveway. He unbuckled his seatbelt. I unbuckled mine. He opened the driver's side door and got out. He opened the passenger door for me. I didn't move. I still needed the assurance. I closed my eyes, preparing to open up to him.

"You know Mya is in the mental health facility. Mia, my other daughter, is in the hospital. She is not responding. A ventilator is keeping her alive."

Tears escaped my closed eyes. I felt Will's fingers wiping the tears away. He gently pulled me out of the passenger's seat. He wrapped his arms around me.

"I'm here for you," he said, kissing my forehead. "Thank you for letting me in. I know that was hard. I'm sorry to hear that. I'm right here anytime you need me."

I believed Will when he said he would be there for me. I was scared and unsure about moving forward with him, but my heart told me he was dependable and trustworthy.

Will

We sat around the conference room table at my firm. We met with another team to partner with a new contract for products. I was reviewing the contract with my assistant, attorney, and lead team engineer. My phone began to ring. It was not my regular ringtone. The tone belonged to Kim. I silenced it and continued to work. It was my lunchtime, and the meeting ran over. I would call her back. The phone began to vibrate. That was awkward. She never called me back-to-back. She would always shoot a text.

"Excuse me," I said, stepping out of the room.

"Hey, Baby," I said, answering the call.

She was upset. She was crying and screaming. All I heard was that she was at the hospital for Mia. I told her I was on my way to her.

I rushed into the waiting room of the hospital. Kim was crying in Allison's arms. I walked over to her and pulled her into my arms.

"They want me to take my baby off life support," she cried.

"What do you want to do?" I asked.

"I want to keep her on," she cried.

"Okay, then you do not have to sign

anything," I said.

She wanted to stay with her daughter. She thought I was going back to work. I told her that I was staying with her. My assistant was able to handle affairs at the office for me.

She sat in a chair next to her daughter's bed. I watched as she cried and cried. She eventually cried herself to sleep. I covered her with a blanket before leaving to meet my mother.

My mother agreed she would keep the children. I headed back to the hospital. After 2 hours, she was sleeping in the chair. I gently rubbed her face, and she opened her eyes.

"You need to rest in bed," I said to her.

"My baby...." she said, tearing up.

"She is going to be fine," I said. "We will come back tomorrow."

I helped her up from the chair. Kim walked over to the hospital bed. She kissed Mia on the cheek. I held the hospital room door open for her. She walked out. I took her hand. We made our way to the elevator. While we rode the elevator down to the parking deck. She rested her head on my chest. I rubbed her back.

I drove her to my house. I did not want her home alone. Her friends understood. They knew they had free access to my house to drop in to check on her.

We both were sitting on the couch in my living room. I wiped each tear as they fell from her face.

"You want to talk?" I asked her.

My question caused her to cry more. I knew it probably would. I was still learning Kim, but I knew her at the same time. She needed to talk.

Kim

It was time for me to tell Will everything. More tears fell down my face.

"My life was perfect. My family was perfect. Everything was perfect. I do not understand what happened. My girls were the perfect angels until high school. Mia started fighting. She had so many write-ups and suspensions. Mya began to shut herself off from the world. The school staff found Mia on the floor of the locker room. She overdosed on pills. Mya tried to commit suicide. Cut her arm up. Mia had never told her side of the story. Mya told the police her side. I get sick to my stomach thinking about her statement. I stood behind the glass and watched her tell the investigators. She was so angry with me. She did not want to talk to me. She still did not talk to me. My husband, their father, molested our daughters. He did it right in our home for years. My girls were fourteen. Mya told them about incidents that happened when they were 10. At that age, they started to develop physical features. I did not even know. How could I miss it? I was the perfect mother. My girls were not supposed to be sexually abused by their dad. I thought I had prevented it. I knew what had happened to my friends, Audrey and Lauren. I told myself I would not allow that to happen to my girls."

Will rubbed his hand down my arm. My head was resting on his chest. I felt him kiss me on my forehead.

"I'm so sorry, Kim," he said.

"I was a great wife to my husband! I did not understand why he did those awful, sickening things to our daughters. I was committed to him! I served him! Anything he ever needed or wanted, I was right there! He was above everything!"

Will stood up from the couch.

Will

I only knew to say to Kim once she finished venting, "We need to pray."

Kim smirked, "Did I mention I dedicated my life to the church? I stayed in God's word. My girls still were molested by their father!"

"The Devil attacks those who believe in and serve God," I said. "We have to remember 1 Peter 5:8. The word tells us to be alert and of sober mind; the Devil looks for us to devour!"

Kim continued to cry. I only knew to pray. I decided to kneel in front of the couch. She did the same. We both then prayed together. I asked God to send down healing and prayed for the renewal of her spirit.

Audrey

For our monthly girls' day outing, we headed for manicures and pedicures! I was excited! I did not know about the girls, but I needed it. We each sat along the wall as our nails dried, enjoying our pedicures and conversation.

Tameka walked into the nail salon with 3 of her friends. I tried not to pay any attention to her. She kept staring at us.

The girls noticed. She was there for a pedicure. She sat down right across from us. While the nail tech filled her tub with water, she kept staring. I thought she was staring at me. After paying close attention to her, I saw her staring at Kim. That was a big mistake.

"Hey!" said Kim to her.

I lowered my head! Lauren shook her head. Allison quickly looked away.

"Kimberly," said Tameka.

Kim eyed her, "You are staring hard. Is there anything I can help you with?"

"There is!" snapped Tameka.

"I'm listening," said Kim.

"You can stay away from Will. He is my man."

Kim laughed. She continued to laugh.

Tameka then said,

"He has been mine since he stepped into Crestview."

Tameka even gave the date the man moved to Crestview. I noticed Kim was no longer laughing. Her demeanor revealed Tameka had the right date! The woman even had the nerve to name his children! I knew we needed to get Kim out of the nail shop. Tameka was not alone. The last thing pastor needed to hear was his first lady, and her friends tore up the nail shop!

Tameka was messy! She had the audacity to pull out her phone! She was being too disrespectful. The girl read text messages plus the man's phone number. Every person in the nail shop was shocked! Kim sat quietly. She allowed the tech to finish her pedicure. She even paid. We were about to head out of the door. Kim turned around and walked toward the pedicure area. Before I knew it, she took a fist full of Tameka's hair and yanked her out of the chair. Kim was wearing Tameka out in the middle of the nail shop. Punch after punch. Tameka couldn't get a hit in if she tried. We rushed over to Kim, trying to pull her away. She was strong!

"Let her hair go!" said Lauren, stepping between the two. Allison had Kim's hand. She was trying her best to open her hand. I was on the other side, holding Kim's free hand. I knew my nails were about to be messed up! We managed to pull her away. She snatched away from us and left the nail shop.

Kim

I was heated! I was angry! Angry was not the word! I was pissed! If my friends had not pulled me away from her, I was going to do some serious damage! How dare she try and blast me in the nail shop! She acted like she did not know who I was! I was nothing like Audrey! I was not about to play games with her!

I called Will before going to his house! I needed to make sure he was there. He and I had planned to spend the evening together after I left the outing with my friends. I wouldn't have been surprised if he was out planning for the evening.

He answered his phone, telling me he was home. That was good! I had some business to handle with him too! He told me the door would be open. That was fine because I was ready to give him his key back!

I pulled into his driveway. I got out of the Audi, slamming the door so hard. He did have the door unlocked. I twisted the knob of the front door and pushed it open. I closed the door behind me. I saw him standing with a gift bag in his living room. He was opening his arms to hug me when I slapped him.

"You sleeping with Tameka? What do y'all have going on?"

"Let me explain," he calmly pleaded.

Oh! I was beyond pissed! I was not looking for him to explain the relationship with Tameka! I was looking for him to tell me he didn't have anything going on with her. Will wanted to explain the situation! Oh! No sir! I was not going to listen to him lie to me!

"No!" I yelled, "She explained everything in the nail shop! In front of everybody! How dare you?"

"I need you to listen to me," he said.

"No! I trusted you! I opened up to you! We are over!" I yelled before leaving his house. I made sure I slammed the door behind me so hard that it rang throughout the house.

Tears filled my eyes as I drove home. They ran down my face as I hit my stirring wheel while parked in my driveway. Once I could get out of my car, I went inside my house. I went to my bedroom and tucked myself under the covers of my bed.

Will was blowing my phone up. My friends were calling too. I didn't even bother to answer. I didn't want to talk to anyone.

My alarm sounded. Someone was downstairs. When I heard my alarm deactivate, I knew it had to be my friends. Sure enough, Lauren pulled the covers back.

"We need to talk to you," she said.

"Well, I need to talk to you," said Allison.

"We are here because we are all friends," said Audrey.

I eyed them and sat up in bed.

Allison sighed. Audrey nudged her to talk. Allison said, "I did not know for sure, but I knew Tameka was with Will."

I could have dived across my bed and close-lined her to the floor. I knew there had to be more to the story. I remained quiet. Allison continued. "It was gossip that I was hearing, and I didn't tell you because I didn't know if it was true."

Audrey said, "You know I have been a victim of gossip here in Crestview."

"Me too," said Lauren.

Audrey sighed. "I told Allison not to say anything to you unless she knew it was true."

I shrugged my shoulders. I didn't care about what they did. I was hurt more by Will's actions.

"I understand," I said to them, "I just want to be by myself."

Audrey then said to me, "We will leave. Before we go, I want you to know that I don't believe Tameka."

"She had his phone number," I yelled, "She had text messages!"

"I know," sighed Audrey.

"I know you were probably rooting for him and in our corner for us to make it, but it's over."

I threw my body back onto my bed and covered myself with the comforter.

Pastor Reynolds

I invited the guys over to watch the game. We were hanging in my man cave. Jeff and Cornelius were at the pool table. I was sitting in my chair watching the game. Will was sitting on the couch. He hadn't said anything to us.

"Will you straight?" asked Cornelius.

"Naw, man," said Will

"What's going on?"

"I don't even know," said Will. "Kim and I were good. She went to the nail shop with the ladies. Something happened with Tameka. Kim said we were over. I'm not giving up on my relationship with her. What Tameka and I had was so long ago. When I first came to Crestview, we tried dating. We didn't work! Tameka got problems."

"Kim will come around," said Cornelius to Will.

"I should have just told her the truth," he said.

I agreed with Will. Out of the men on the boat, he and I knew Tameka well. Tameka was the possessive type of woman. She struggled with letting go. Not only that, but she also envied other women that had what she thought she should have. I was so glad I dodged that bullet. Tameka had a lot of things to work on before she could be with any man.

"You should have told her from the beginning," I said.

"Yeah, but I did not think things would get to this," said Will, "Especially with Tameka! Most of all, with Kim!"

" I understand what you're saying. I would have told Kim once I began developing feelings for her."

"You are right," he agreed, "I did not think women around here were like that."

I don't believe any of us intentionally laughed on purpose.

"Welcome to Crestview!" said Jeffery.

"Kim tried to tell me," said Will.

Cornelius then said, "The women are from here! We are not! We gotta listen to them."

I had to agree with him. Audrey tried to warn me as well. I did not want to listen. I had to find out the hard way. Cornelius did as well. He faced gossip about pursuing a married woman. He still faced it after she was divorced, married him, and birthed his child! Now, Will was facing the gossip of dating two women at the same time.

Jeffery gave his advice. "Give her time, give her space. I know, Kim! She and Allison are best friends. She is going to come around."

"This is Kim we're talking about," I laughed.

Will had to laugh, "Mane, Kim slapped me so hard!"

"Now, that's Kim," I laughed.

Cornelius laughed, "Bro! I do not even want Kim to go off on me! Ever!"

Will continued to laugh, "Get off, my lady!"

Cornelius held his hands up while laughing. Jeff took his shot on the table. I focused back on the game. I had a feeling Will and Kim were going to work things out.

Will

I blew my horn as I sat outside of my mother's house. I was picking her up for church. I enjoyed Temple of Heaven so much that I invited her to visit. She was in search of a church home.

I opened the church's front door for my family, and they walked in. We sat together in the middle of the congregation. My mother enjoyed the choir. She clapped her hands, tapped her feet, and even waved her hands from time to time. Ryleigh always loved the choir. Junior was fascinated with the music. I looked forward to the sermon. I listened as Daniel introduced his sermon topic. Ryleigh interrupted my concentration by tapping on my leg.

"What is it, sweetheart?" I asked her.

She pointed and said, "Can I go sit with Dr. Kim?"

I slowly looked in the direction she was pointing. Kim was actually at church. I had not spoken to her in a while. Our group session was off for a break.

"You can go," I said to Ryleigh.

She jumped down from the pew and walked to the other right section where Kim was. Kim picked her up, and they embraced one another. I redirected my attention back to Daniel when he delivered the scripture he would be preaching from,

"Exodus 20:3-5"

Pastor Reynolds

My sermon topic was one that I had visited before. I visited it twice before. Each one came from a different scripture. Each one had a different message but a similar topic. The sermon topic this time was,

"The Recipe of A Godly Woman: Perfection. She Serves One God. He Reigns Over Man."

Men can be fascinated with things just as a woman can. These things can be items. Items can be video games, clothing, shoes, and even money. You may not like it when the car gets too dirty from driving it. He may find himself washing it every week. Women, you may have to have that new Dooney and Burke or Brahmin purse that you did not see in the store last time, but you see it this time. It may not be things. It can be an organization, a job, or a social club. It may be a physical feature. Women, you love your hair. Your bundles must always be on point! That unit must fit right. My daughters often tell me they can't get the hair that sheds!

You may want to have body surgery to fit into society's view. We see it every day with celebrities. We can be so fascinated with things that we forget

THE RECIPE OF A GODLY WOMAN IV

about God. We forget God blessed us with the car, clothes on our backs, the money in our pockets, or the money in that Dooney and Burke or Brahmin purse. We even sometimes forget the Bible tells us in Genesis that God made us in his image. He did not make us in the image of how others want to see us. He did not make us in the image of how you want to see yourself.

We can also be fascinated with a person. Fascination can be forced or lustful. Men and women can be so fascinated with their partners that they will do anything to keep them. Not only will they do anything to keep them, but they will do whatever to keep a smile on their face. The man or woman finds themselves worshiping the person or serving the person. Fascination, worshiping or serving another more than you worship or serve God is not His word. In the book of James, we learned we could be tempted when we are turned away from God by the Devil, enticing us with our own desires. We also know that the book of Galatians tells us that if we walk by the spirit, we will not gratify our desires of the flesh.

The devil will use any force to get you off track. He will make that person look so good that anyone will forget God's commandant of "thou shalt have no other gods before me."

They will forget he said, "Thou shalt not bow down thyself to them, nor serve them: for I the Lord thy God am a jealous God."

When the Devil begins to work, chaos begins

in the lives of those who were blinded by him. That is his mission. He wants to stir up the lives of those who are true worshipers and servants of God.

Audrey

Just like with any other sermon, my husband began to tell a story. He told the story of a woman. The woman was a true worshiper and servant of God. She did His will inside of the church and inside of her home. However, her husband did not believe the same as she did. They were unevenly yoked. She married the man, and they began to live life. She was fascinated with her new life. She felt it was perfect. Her children were born! She felt they were perfect! She had the perfect family. She was fascinated with perfection, forgetting that no man is perfect. The woman was so fascinated with her husband that she began to forget about her duty to serve God. The Devil was working! The Devil had her just where he wanted her. He snuck into her home and destroyed her family. The destruction could have been prevented, but the woman even forgot how to pray. She forgot how to seek God in times of trouble. Her family was destroyed, and she did not know what to do.

Even in our darkest times, God will send us an angel. He sent her an angel. He did not send the angel for the woman to be fascinated. He sent her an angel to reveal to her you are not alone. He sent her a praying partner. The woman did not know it. She was still consumed in the web of the Devil, and he was wrapping her tighter. God used man to reveal to her some things. God wanted her to see she had forgotten who He was. He wanted her to know that even in her darkest time, He would be there. He wanted her to know it was time to come back to Him. She was not hearing the word of God. Finally, she heard the word of God; she was able to go to God in prayer with the angel. The Devil did not like that. He began to work through others. He got her off guard again. She was right where he wanted her. The Devil did not want her to be happy. He does not want us to be happy. He wants us to remain in sin.

Even though he wants us to remain in sin, we do not have to stay there. God sent His son to die for our sins. We also have to work. We have to pray and give our burdens over to Him. My husband ended the sermon with this,

"We have to confess that He is the only true God that can make us whole again. Not a person, place, or thing. We have to serve only Him and follow His word."

Kim

Being back in the church felt good. I dealt with the looks and stares. I had to remind myself I was not there for them. I was there for myself. I really did not want to go that day, but I am glad I decided to go. I needed that sermon from my pastor.

The next day, I stopped by the hospital to see my baby. I stood on the side of the hospital bed, staring at my daughter. She was still on life support. Doctors gave up hope. They were waiting on me to sign to remove her. I could not do that. As I stared at her, I began to think about the sermon Daniel had preached.

I went straight home after my visit. I headed up to my room. I kneeled down on the side of my bed. I closed my eyes, and I began my prayer with, "God, I know that you are the only one that can make me whole again."

Mya

My fifteenth birthday was here! For some reason, I woke up excited! Any girl spending her fifteenth birthday in a mental health facility would not have been happy, but I was. I was ready to see my mother! I normally did not want to see her! This time it was different! Something had come over me. Something I could not explain.

I was in my room when the escort came. I anxiously rushed to the door. I heard the woman say, "Mya, your mother is here to see you." That felt so good to hear. I smiled so big.

When the door to the visitation room opened, I ran out of it. I stopped at the sight of my mom with my favorite-colored balloons, ice cream, cake, and gifts. I ran to her and gave her a hug. I knew she was shocked. I hugged her so tight and waited for her to wrap her arms around me. She started to cry before she squeezed me tight.

I normally sat across from her. During this visit, I sat next to her and took the tissue from the box sitting on the table. I wiped her face.

"Mama, I want to say that I am sorry."

I had to apologize. I blamed her for my father molesting and raping me and my sister. I blamed

THE RECIPE OF A GODLY WOMAN IV

her, and I knew that was not right. I wanted to apologize for my actions toward her since she had been coming to see me. I wanted her to know that I was not just apologizing because it was my birthday. I apologized because it was the right thing to do. When she accepted my apology, I hugged her again. She kissed me on my forehead. She had something to say.

"I accept your apology. I want you to know that I have made sure that your father is receiving the right consequences for what he did to you. I also want you to know that I am going to make sure you and your sister are never hurt again."

I had to cry. Dealing with the hurt, pain, nightmares, and suicidal thoughts had been a struggle for me. Just as they had been a struggle for me, I knew my mother was hurting too.

"I remember when we were little?" I said to her. "You taught us how to pray. You would pray with us. Then you stopped when we got older. I thought about those times. I started praying. Mama, I prayed to God by myself."

A smile was on her face. She grabbed my hands, telling me she was proud of me.

"Don't ever stop praying," said Mama.

"Yes, ma'am. I will always pray.'

I had to ask about my sister. My mama lowered her head. I knew things were not good,

"Pray for her, too," she said to me.

"I have. I won't stop," I said.

"She is still on life support. The doctors want

me to take her off."

I begged my Mama not to sign for Mia to be removed from life support. She said that she was not taking my sister off life support. I believed her.

The birthday cake was so good! The ice cream was way better than the ice cream cups we were given in the facility. I loved my gifts, new clothes, shoes, and a journal.

My behavior improved at the facility. I was able to go outside. I was not able to go at first. I was a high risk of running. My mama and I walked outside along a path. I was curious about something.

"Mama, when you first started to come to visit, you weren't really yourself. You did not even look like yourself. You wore your hair in a ponytail. You had on scrubs or sweats. Then there were times when you looked like yourself! Your hair was pretty. The Make-up was flawless. Your outfit was cute! Then it stopped, and you went back to the ponytails, sweats, and scrubs. Kind of how you are now. What happened to the happy you? I know you were not happy with dad and what happened with us, but you were, and now it's gone again."

Kim

I stopped walking. I had to look at myself. My daughter was right. I was back to being just Kim. I then tried to find a way to explain things to her.

"I have been going to therapy too," I said to her, beginning to walk down the path again.

"It could not have been working at first," she said.

I laughed and said, "I was not giving it a chance at first."

She laughed. "Sorry. I am just saying! When you did give it a chance, that must have been the time you were all dressed up and happy?"

Her question made me stop walking. I eyed her. She eyed me back. *I knew why I was eyeing her. She did not know why I was eyeing her. Was God speaking to me through my child?*

"It was," I answered her.

Mya then folded her arms. She examined me from head to toe. "Did you give up again?" *God was using my child to speak to me.*

"I never gave him time to explain himself," I said.

"What?" asked Mya, "Him? What, Mama?"

"Nothing, sweetie," I said.

Mia

I heard a voice. It did not know the voice. It sounded like they were praying. I knew my mother's voice. It was not her. I knew my sister's voice. It was not her. It was not my aunt Audrey, Lauren, or Allison. It had to be my uncle Daniel. I knew for sure it was him praying. I opened my eyes. It was not my uncle. I did not know who the man was. He said, "Amen," and opened his eyes.

He was staring at me, and I was staring at him. He did not say a word. He smiled and left out of the door.

I was in a hospital bed. I had no idea why I was there. I had no idea how I got there. I only knew one thing. I wanted my mama. There was a remote-type thing on the side of me. I pressed the button that had the nurse symbol on it. Four nurses rushed into my room. One of them said, "Oh my God! It is a miracle!"

"Where is my Mama?" I asked them.

Audrey

When I received the phone call, I began to shout! God answered our prayers! He was an awesome God! Mya was ready to be released from the mental health facility. Kim needed us to help her move Mya back home! We were there when she was admitted. We told her we would be there to help bring her home. My husband and I drove our SUV. Lauren and Cornelius were not too far behind us. Allison, of course, was right there for her best friend! We were a family! We never allowed one of us to face any trial or tribulation alone.

Mya came running out of the facility toward us as we got out of our vehicles. She dashed to her aunt Allison first. Lauren and I were next, and she then embraced her mom. I tried to stop my tears of joy from falling! It was a wonderful feeling to see the two reunited.

We worked together to move her things from the facility and into our vehicles. She was busy saying goodbye to the friends she had made. Allison came back inside from taking a bag to her car. She was holding her phone. She rushed over to me.

"Where is Kim?"

"She is in Mya's room."

"I have the doctor from the hospital on the phone."

Once everything was loaded, we stood outside of the facility. Allison needed to talk to Kim. "Where is your phone?" she asked her. Kim looked at us all. She then said, "I left it in the car. Why?"

"The hospital called," said Allison. "They could not reach you, so they called me."

"It's about my baby, huh?" asked Kim eyeing Allison.

Allison then said, "She woke up."

Mya grabbed Kim. They hugged each other so tight. Kim thanked God over and over again. He showed up right on time!

Kim

Mya beat me through the hospital doors, to the elevator, and to her sister's room. She pushed the door open. She stopped at the sight of Mia sitting up in the hospital bed. Mia slowly turned to face her sister. They stared at one another.

Mya rushed over to the bed. She hugged her sister. It did not take long for my girls to share tears. I could not stop my tears from falling. I joined them. I held my girls so tight. I was forever thankful to God for bringing them both back to me. We were going to be a family again. I needed my girls; I knew they needed me. We all needed God to come into our lives to heal and restore. I prayed right then and there with my girls.

Mia was not released immediately. The doctor wanted to make sure her body was functioning properly. The doctor wanted to monitor her for 48 hours. Mya wanted to stay. I did not make her leave. I wanted to stay. I decided to head home and bring us some clothes back.

My girls were laughing as they entertained one another when I walked back into the room with overnight bags for us each. I did not want to interrupt. I smiled and made my way over to the other side of the room.

Mya then said, "Mama, bring your chair over here so you can watch the movie with us! It's about to come on!"

I smiled, moving my chair to the opposite side of the hospital bed. The three of us enjoyed A Wrinkle In Time. They soon fell asleep after the movie finished. I gently covered Mia in the hospital bed and Mya on the roll-out bed. I was happy to have my babies together again.

I shouted to the heavens when the nurse came in two days later and informed us Mia was going to be discharged that day! Mya immediately began to help me pack her things! I knew she was ready to begin to live a new life! I knew Mia was, and I was more than ready!

I called my friends. They came to help us move Mia just like they showed up to help me with Mya. Her uncles made sure her things got down to the car. Her aunties helped me get her out of bed. They made sure to follow us home.

As I drove down the street, I heard Mya say, "Mama, where are we going? This is not the way to our house."

"We have a new house," I said to her.

"Really!" they both said in sync.

Those were definitely my girls! They were back!

"I felt you all would need a new start when you came home. I moved out of that house a while ago."

"You did that for us?" asked Mya.

I smiled. "I did, baby girl."

"Thank you, Mama," said Mia, "That means a lot to us."

Our old home would have opened old wounds. I did not want that for my girls. Our home was the main place where the abuse occurred. I was not going to force them to move back there. I also tore it to pieces. I could not tell them I needed a new start too.

They loved the new house! The minute I pulled into the driveway, they went bananas! They beat me out of the car as if they had a key! I opened the front door, and they rushed inside. It did not take them long to find the staircase. They were looking for their rooms! I knew when they found them. I did not bother to go upstairs. I listened at the bottom of the staircase.

"Mama! My room is so pretty!" yelled Mya.

"A canopy bed!" yelled Mia.

My heart was warm! It was seconds from melting. I leaned against the wall. I looked up and said, "Thank you, God."

My friends walked into the home with Mia's things. They could hear the joy coming from upstairs. Audrey placed her hand over her mouth. I knew she was holding back tears. Lauren smiled. Allison walked over to me. I fell into my best friend's arms crying tears of joy.

Audrey

I stood in the choir stand singing as church service was beginning. I saw Kim and her daughters come into the sanctuary. I smiled. It was great to see them back. After services, my family greeted the members and guests. Kim and her girls were in line. I hugged them. Ariel and Layla came running to the twins. They missed their cousins so much. Mya hugged Ariel so tight! She was her favorite. Mia picked up Layla. Layla hugged her neck. Lauren popped up on the side of me. We shared a long hug. She then hugged Kim. Allison came, hugging her best friend so tight. We all were happy to see her there.

After church, we invited everyone over for Sunday dinner. The plan was for the ladies to cook and for the guys to enjoy football while the kids entertained themselves. We came together every once in a while for Sunday dinner. We often left Sundays for each of us to enjoy time with our families. Everyone accepted the invitation

Kim

It was time for group therapy to start again. I was nervous about going. I knew I would have to face Will. I was torn! I knew I did not give him a chance to explain himself. I was ready to be a woman and hear him out.

His car was not in the parking lot of the building where the session was held. I figured he was late. The session had been in for an hour. He still had not come. We did not break off into groups that day. I was happy. My partner was not there. I would not have got anywhere.

The next day, his car still was not in the parking lot. I was beginning to wonder about him. I was not focused on the session that day. I wondered where he was. My thoughts were interrupted when he walked into the session. My heart dropped. I stopped breathing for a second at the sight of him. I immediately redirected my focus to the facilitator. She told us to prepare for our individual groups. As I was getting up from my chair, I heard her say, "Kim, you have a new partner."

I lost my hearing after that. I did not even know who she said my new partner was. I stood in the middle of the floor. She placed her hand on my shoulder, "Kim, did you hear me?"

"Who did you say again?" I asked her.

She told me who my new partner was. I still was not paying attention. I sat down with the person that was not sitting with anyone. I did not talk!

Mia

My sister and I were watching the kids play in the backyard. I was thirsty. I headed into the house to get something to drink. I walked into the kitchen. My mother and aunties were cooking! It smelled good. As I opened the refrigerator to get a bottle of water, I heard a little girl.

"Dr. Kim!" she said.

I saw a little dark girl run to my mother. I did not recognize her. I closed the refrigerator door. *There was a tall, dark man standing there. I was looking at him, and he was looking at me. I thought I knew him from somewhere. I did not say anything. It was kind of awkward.* I went back outside.

Mya

My sister came back outside. She handed me water. Two kids came out of the house right after she did. I did not know them. Apparently, they knew our cousins. Ariel and Layla were playing with the little girl like they had done this before. Lil Greg and Jeff Jr. were playing with the little boy like he belonged! I looked over at my sister, and she shrugged her shoulders. Yeah, we were lost or had been gone for too long!

Dinner was awkward! My family was tripping! Everyone was quiet! I knew something was off! All you could hear was forks hitting plates! At least that meant the food was good.

After dinner, I sat in the den. I wanted to watch everybody. Something was up! My aunties were playing spades at the table. My uncles were shooting pool. The kids were playing connect four, and my sister was scrolling all in her phone. I saw the new little girl get down from her chair at the connect four table and walk over to where my aunties were playing spades. She tapped my mother's leg. She knew my mama!

"Dr. Kim," said the little girl. "Can I come over your house?"

THE RECIPE OF A GODLY WOMAN IV

She had been to our new house! Who was this little girl? How did she know my mama?

Mama got up from the table with the little girl. She came over to where I was sitting and sat down. The little girl climbed in her lap like my sister, and I did when we were little. I smiled at her. The little girl buried her face into my mom's chest.

"It's okay," said Mama, rubbing her back. "You do not have to be shy. I know this big girl. This is my little girl Mya."

My mama then pointed at my sister. "She is my little girl too. Her name is Mia."

We both waved at the little girl. She slowly waved back at us. I could tell she was shy.

"You want to tell them your name?" my mama asked her.

"My name is Ryleigh," she said.

The little girl never left my mother's side. She reminded me of Mia when we were little! Stuck all up my mother's behind! She followed my Mama into the kitchen. She wanted ice cream. I heard my mother tell her to ask her father.

I followed the little girl. She went right over to the new dark-skinned man. His response was, "If it's okay with Kim, it's okay with me."

I had to tilt my head to the side! My nosey radar went off! First of all, he was her father. I did not see her mother. Why did it matter what my mama said? I sat back on the couch, continuing to peep the scene. I saw the man take out his phone. Minutes later, my Mama's phone beeped. She had a

131

text message. I watched as she placed it on vibrate before she texted back. The man looked back at his phone. *They were texting each other!*

I watched as my mother pulled my Aunt Allison outside. When they came back inside, she came over to me and said,

"Aunt Allison is going to take you and your sister back to her house for a while."

I was okay with it. I had a feeling us going to her house had something to do with that text message.

Kim

The text message Will sent me said we needed to talk. I didn't know why he wanted to talk. If I were honest with myself, I was glad he wanted to talk to me. I did not care why we needed to talk. My girls headed with Allison after dinner. Will allowed his children to stay with Audrey and Daniel. He wanted me to meet him at the west side café. I did. We arrived at the same time. He held the door open for me. He hadn't said much. He went to place an order. I found a booth. I did not understand why he was ordering when we had just had dinner and dessert. He came over to the booth with two cups of chocolate ice cream. I smiled.

"I hope you are not too full for chocolate ice cream."

"Never," I laughed.

"I have to go back home," he said. "The trial is going to start."

"For the rape of Ryleigh and the molestation of Junior?" I asked him.

He gave a nod. He had to leave early. His worse fear was going to happen. The prosecuting attorney was going to place his children on the stand to testify. He did not want that. The attorney needed to prep the children.

"I don't think Ryleigh will be able to do it," he said, lowering his head.

"She's a strong little girl."

"I talked to the kids about going back home. She wants to stay here."

I lowered my head. I knew Ryleigh was a gentle and sweet little girl. I knew she did not handle the news well.

"Junior wants to stay too."

I could not help but think about how angry he became when Will broke the news to him. He was doing so well with his anger.

"Junior doesn't want to leave my mom. She was there when I told them. She is willing to come with us."

I was there as a listening ear for him. He needed to vent and get things off his chest.

"Ryleigh does not want to leave you," he said to me.

I slowly raised my head and made direct eye contact with him.

"When my mom told Junior she would be coming with us; she asked could you come."

My heart fell completely out of my body. I had no response for him. I could not gather myself. Tears came, and before I knew it, they were rushing down my face. I got up from the table and left the café.

Will

I called for Kim to come back, but she did not. I got up from the table and tried to catch her. She was already out of the door. By the time I got to the door, she was in her car. She left.

Audrey opened the door of her house. I wondered if Kim was there. She told me she was not. She then called Allison. Allison said she was not there. Daniel, Audrey, and I sat in their living room with Allison on the speakerphone. We were trying to figure out where she could be. They asked me to tell them what had happened, and I told them. Allison then said, "Audrey...."

Audrey looked at the phone and said, "Yeah, I know where she is. I'll direct him."

I had only been on the west side of Crestview for the café. It was different, but it appeared buildings and homes were being renovated. I followed the directions Audrey gave me. I pulled onto the parking lot of the park on that side, and there was Kim's car. I parked my car and got out. I continued to follow Audrey's direction. There definitely was a path. I followed it. I stopped at the gorgeous site of a sunflower field. Even though it was dark, it was still just as beautiful. I only wanted to see it in the daytime. Kim was sitting on a nearby stump, staring out at the flowers.

"Hey," I said to her.

She did not bother to look my way. More tears poured down her face. She lowered her head and covered her face.

"I do not know what I said to trigger you," I said to her. "I want to apologize."

"It's not you," she said to me.

I felt as though she needed to talk. I walked over to her and pulled her up from the stomp. "Then tell me what is wrong."

"My ex-husband, he rapped and molested our twin girls."

Kim did not attend the trial. She was emotionally unstable. Her doctor did not recommend it. Her ex-husband was found guilty. She was pleased with the verdict. She was not pleased with her actions. She felt she let her daughters down by not paying attention to recognize the abuse. She felt she added salt to their wounds when she did not attend the trial. All of Crestview knew what had happened. Many individuals were asking how could she not show up for her daughters.

She then said to me, "Before you and I started dating, Ryleigh was my girl. Once we started dating, she and I became close. Since we ended, all I have thought about was her. I was happy to introduce her to my girls."

"What else?" I asked her trying to

understand her.

"I remember when my girls were her age. She has to grow up." I watched her as she lowered her head. "I don't want to let her down too." She covered her face and burst into tears.

Kim

He pulled my hands from my face. He lifted my chin and wiped my face. He then said to me, "Kim, you are not perfect. You heard the sermon Daniel delivered. You can't fix everything. Some things you have to allow God to fix. The guilt you are holding on to, you have to give it over to God."

"You are right," I said to him. "Everything I gave to Him, He has worked a miracle. There are two things I have not gone to Him about."

"You need to," he said to me. "Not for your girls, not for my children, not for me, but for you."

I could have prayed with Will right then and there. I could have called Audrey to pray with me. I could have called Lauren to pray with me. My best friend would have loved to be my prayer partner. Before each session with my pastor, we prayed. I could have called on him. I did not call any of them. I knew I had to go to God alone. I had to give everything to Him. Sometimes Christians feel if we give one or two things to Him, he will fix everything. True enough, God knows everything. We must fully give Him all our trials and tribulations, not pieces. I gave Him pieces the last time. The next time, I would give Him every situation.

Will sat down on the stump. He eased me down in his lap. He wrapped his arms around me. I leaned back into his arms. He kissed me on the cheek while I stared out at the sunflowers.

After leaving the field of sunflowers, he trailed me to make sure I made it safely. He didn't come in. I got out of my car and went into the house. Once I was inside, I watched him leave my driveway from my living room window. Allison was on her way with the girls. I remembered the time Will and I prayed at his house. I kneeled in front of my couch. I started to pray. I prayed for peace. I needed a renewed mind, heart, and spirit. I let go of my guilt. I gave my fears to God. I was ready to trust Him fully. I was willing to accept any and every blessing He had in store for me.

Will

My family and I sat in a small room inside the courthouse. My lawyer was reviewing last-minute information with me and my mother about the case before the trial began. My children sat quietly. I knew they were nervous. They may have been afraid. I was nervous. I did not want to see their mother's boyfriend. I did not know how I was going to react. I asked to be excused. I needed to pray. My mother had already prayed over my children that morning. I found a small room not too far from where we were. I closed the door, and I began to pray for a positive attitude, adequate tolerance, strength, and the ability to forgive.

The trial was about to start. The lawyer escorted my family and me to the elevator that led to the courtroom. We took the elevator down to the first floor. We stepped off the elevator. Ryleigh was holding my hand. All of a sudden, she let go of my hand. I turned around to see her running. Kim kneeled and hugged her. I smiled. I was glad she was there for Ryleigh.

Kim asked her, "How are you feeling?"

Ryleigh fell into her arms. Kim held my baby close. We both knew Ryleigh was nervous. Kim went into her purse.

"Look who I brought," she said, pulling Yaya the puppet from her purse.

Ryleigh smiled so big. Kim pulled a stuffed lamb from her purse, handing it to Ryleigh. "Look what else I have."

Ryleigh took the lamb and held it. "Another Yaya," she said.

"Your own, Yaya," said Kim. "I talked to some very important people here. They said you can take your Yaya with you when you talk in front of the people today."

"I can?" asked Ryleigh.

"Yes, you can," said Kim. "If you get scared, you can hug or squeeze your Yaya."

"Okay," smiled Ryleigh.

Kim then said, "You now have your daddy, grandma, and Yaya here for you."

Ryleigh hugged her. "I have you too."

Kim hugged her back. "Yes, you have me here too."

I walked over to them with my hands in my pocket. Kim looked up at me. Our eyes locked. Mine glazed over for a second.

Kim

I stood, accepting a full hug from Will. He held me for a minute. He kissed me on the cheek. He thanked me for coming. He whispered in my ear. "She needed you."

"You're welcome. I was not going to miss it," I whispered back. I looked down at Ryleigh. She took my hand. She smiled, holding her Yaya in the other hand. We entered the courtroom filled with individuals holding hands. I later learned the case turned into a high-profile case due to the magnitude of abuse. One of the reasons Will moved his children.

Will sat with the prosecuting attorney. We sat behind them. Ryleigh sat next to me. I noticed a woman sitting across from her. I knew she was their mother. Ryleigh favored her. She looked our way. She called out to her daughter. Ryleigh moved closer to me. I felt as though it was only appropriate that she spoke back to her mother. Regardless of the situation, she was still her mother. I took Ryleigh by her hand and walked her over to the woman.

"Hey honey," said the woman as tears filled her eyes.

Ryleigh lowered her head. I bent down to whisper in her ear. She almost jumped into my arms.

"It's okay," I whispered. "You can say hello to your mother."

Ryleigh loosened her grasp around my neck. She waved at her mother. "Hey, Mama."

Tears began to run down her mother's face. Junior then came over. He waved and said, "Hey, Mama." He eased closer to me. I wrapped my other arm around him.

"Hey, son," she cried.

She then said to me, "You must be Kim."

I wondered how she knew my name. "Yes, I am."

Their mother thanked me for letting the kids speak to her. "The last time I saw them, child protective services were taking them from me. Thank you for taking care of my children."

I wondered how she knew I was caring for Junior and Ryleigh. With the thoughts consuming me, I was still able to say, "You're welcome."

The prosecuting attorney called Ryleigh to testify first. She got down from my lap. The attorney led her to the witness seat. I was so nervous for her. As the attorney began to ask her questions about the abuse Will caught my attention. He was fidgeting with a pin. I knew he was becoming angry. I prayed before I made it to the trial. I asked God to give him the strength he needed to make it through the day. He was very strong for his daughter. He made it through her testimony.

The trial lasted two days. I stayed in a hotel not too far from the hotel where Will and his family were. At the conclusion of the trial, the jury found the defendant guilty of first-degree rape. He was sentenced to life in prison. Will was granted full custody of his children.

I was packing my things to leave my hotel and head back home when my phone began to ring. Will was calling. He asked if he could stop by.

There were several knocks at my hotel door. There was no need to ask who it was. I knew it was him. I opened the door.

"Hey," he said, standing with his hands in his pockets.

"Hey," I said, stepping aside so that he could come inside. I closed the door behind him.

"Are you about to head back?"

"I am," I said.

"Thank you for coming and staying the entire time," he said.

I smiled and said, "You're welcome."

"We need to talk," he said.

I agreed, thinking about the time I did not allow him to explain himself. He then said, "I wanted to talk at Sunday dinner. I had this trial on my mind. I did not know how you would respond. Ryleigh wanted you there. I did not bring us up because I did not want to make you upset to the point that you decided not to talk to me." He reached out for my hands and gently took them into his. My heart began to beat so fast. I had to admit I was not ready for the truth, but my heart was going to accept it.

He then said, "Baby, Kimberly."

Lord, that man had not called me baby or by my first name in months! I almost melted!

"I should have told you this from the beginning. Tameka and I did date. She and I dated when I first came to Crestview. My first project was to do renovations for the doctor's office where she works."

From the time he began to do renovations in the office, Tameka started to flirt with him. That sounded familiar. She constantly threw herself at him. That sounded like Tameka. He finally gave in, and the two started to date. He learned she was jealous. He learned she liked to keep up drama and mess. Tameka had not changed one bit. He did not want to be with a woman like that. He knew she was not going to be a great example for Ryleigh.

"Those were old text messages," he said to me.

"I believe you," I said to him.

He smiled at me. He kissed my hand. I had a question for him.

"Your ex-wife, she knew my name. How does she know about me?"

"She tried to come back into my life. I knew it was only the Devil. I wanted to tell her no. Instead, I found myself telling her I only wanted to be you.

That is how she found out your name."

My heart skipped a million beats. I held my head down. He lifted my chin.

"I miss you. I want us to start over. This time I won't wait to tell you things."

I smiled and said, "We can act like we never left."

Will leaned down, kissing me. I wrapped my arms around his neck, kissing my man back.

Will

My children were fully mine! I was thankful to God. My mother was in great health and spirits! I was thankful to God. Kim and I were back on great terms. I was thankful to God. I was looking forward to moving forward with her. I knew we would have to take things slow because of our children and their abuse. I was prepared for that. I also did not want to rush her. I decided to allow things to work themselves out.

There was one thing I needed to discuss with her. My mother was more than happy to pick the kids up from school. I invited her over after work. She dropped her girls off with Allison and came right over. She was still in her scrubs. She told me she could stay for a little while before she had to pick the girls up. We sat down on my couch. I lifted her legs one by one and placed them in my lap. I removed her shoes and began to massage her feet.

"That feels so good. Thank you. Don't do too much of that. I might fall asleep. I told Allison I would not be too long."

"That is why we need to talk," I said to her.

"About Allison?"

"About your girls?"

"What about them?"

I felt it was time for me to meet them. I felt that if I met them, she would not have to constantly drop them off at Allison's house or wait for them to babysit. I knew she worried about them every time they were out of her sight since they had been home. She would always call to check on them or text. I wanted her to be relieved. I wanted my children to spend time with them. I wanted us all to spend time with one another. I felt they needed to know I would be in their lives. They were old enough.

Kim was blushing by the time I finished explaining myself. I rubbed my finger down her cheek and kissed her hand.

I had an idea. "I tell you what, "I'll start dinner. You can go pick up your girls. I'll have my mom drop off Junior and Ryleigh. We can spend the evening together. That way, you don't have to leave early."

Kim smiled at me. "Okay, that will be fine."

I leaned over and kissed her. She kissed me back without hesitation.

My mom had just brought Junior and Ryleigh home when we heard our front door opening.

"We're in the kitchen," I called out.

Kim and the girls walked into the kitchen. Ryleigh jumped down from the table and ran to Kim. Kim hugged her. I could tell her girls apart. I watched as Mya folded her arms. The observant twin.

"He is cooking," she said. "We went home and changed into something comfortable, and mama would not tell us where we were going."

Kim laughed and shook her head. "We will talk over dinner."

"Yes, ma'am," she laughed.

I tried to start a little bonding with the girls, "Nice to see you all again. My name is Will. Your mom has told me much about you."

"Nice to meet you," they both said.

"We have not heard much about you," snickered Mia, "I think we know why."

Mya burst into laughter. They were characters! Just like Kim!

Kim laughed and asked, "Are you going to help cook or not?"

The girls laughed. Mya then said, "I will help"

Mia wanted to play games with my children. While preparing the dinner, Mya and I began to talk. I was hoping Mia was getting to know Junior and Ryleigh.

"What are some fun things you like to do?" I asked her.

Mya then said, "I like to draw and paint."

She told me she liked to draw and paint nature scenes. She liked to sit outside and paint the trees and the birds. She would even take pictures from the internet or out of a magazine and re-create them. If there were no animals, she would add animals. If there were animals, she would either add more or take them from the scene and add more detail to it. I could tell she was creative. I was even interested in seeing her work.

"Before I left to go to the facility, I would paint and draw with Ariel," she smiled.

I smiled, "Well, you can add another little person to the crew. Ryleigh likes to draw too."

She smiled and said, "Okay. Ariel would love that."

"Has your mom taught you and your sister how to drive? Do you drive yet?" I asked.

Mya burst into laughter, "What! No! Mama's nerves are too bad."

"Do you want to drive?" I asked her.

"Yes! Why would I not want to learn how to drive? We will be sixteen next year!"

"You make good grades?" I asked her

"My sister and I both are geniuses!" she said.

"Keep up the good grades, learn how to drive, and you'll get that permit," I said to her.

"About those last two!" she laughed, "Who is going to teach us, and what car are we going to drive to get the permit? Mama is not letting us behind the wheel of either Audi!"

I laughed at her, "We will work on those two."

She eyed me and said, "We! So, are you saying you're going to be around next year, or am I jumping way ahead of the discussion for dinner?"

She was a smart teenager. I was stuck on what to say. I watched as she folded her arms, eyed me, and tapped her foot as she waited for me to respond.

"We'll discuss it at another time," I said to her.

She held out her hand for me to shake it. I knew where she was headed. She was pretty darn smart! Too smart for me!

"Deal," I said, shaking her hand.

She smiled and said, "Deal."

Kim

We sat at the table eating dinner. The chicken spaghetti with a salad and garlic stick was great! Will and Mya did a fabulous job! Will eyed me. I knew why. I took a deep breath and nodded that I agreed with him talking to the children. He cleared his throat and asked,

"Did everyone enjoy themselves this evening?"

Of course, Ryleigh responded first,

"Yes! Mia is so fun! We played all the games!"

"You will have more fun with me," said Mya," winking at Mia.

Mia laughed, and Ryleigh said, "Well, you both look alike. I will have fun with you too."

I understood what my girl was saying! I had to laugh. Will did as well.

Mya then said, "I draw and paint."

Ryleigh immediately turned to Mya, "You do! Ariel does too! I do too!"

"I do," smiled Mya.

"Well, can both of you just be my favorite twin?"

She melted my entire heart! Mya grabbed her heart and said, "Yes! We both can be your favorite!

Since we look alike!"

Everyone started laughing at the table.

Will then said, "Kim and I are happy you all are getting along well. We were going to talk to you about all of us spending more time together."

"We're listening," smiled Mya.

"How do you all feel about that?"

"I like you," said Mya, "If that's what you're asking."

I laughed and said, "Answer the question, smarty pants."

"I like you too," said Mia to Will, "I mean, I'm just saying. If it helps any."

I laughed and said to her, "You too, smarty pants! Answer the question."

Ryleigh then said, "I already like Dr. Kim!" Junior added, "Me too!"

Mia and Mya started to laugh! Mia, who was drinking her lemonade, had to catch it from spilling out of her mouth. Mya then said, "Even the little ones get it," giving me a wink! Will smiled at me from across the table. I was blushing! My girls were very smart! I knew it was not going to take them long to figure out Will and I were dating.

The cheesecake came after dinner, plus a movie. After the movie, my girls and I headed home. When I made it home, they headed for the shower. I made my way to my backyard. I was sitting outside in my lounging chair, thinking about my future with Will and my family intertwining with his. My patio door opened, and Mya came out.

"Hey, Sweetness," I said to her.

She kissed me on the cheek and sat down in the other chair next to me.

"Is Will the reason why you were all happy and dressed up when you came to see me at the facility?" she asked.

There was no need for me to lie to my daughter. She was very mature and very observant.

"He was," I replied.

She smiled and asked me, " He was the man that you did not allow to explain himself?"

"He was," I replied.

"You must have let him explain himself because you let us meet him," she said to me.

"I did," I said to her.

She smiled and said, "Mama, me and Mia know that daddy hurt you like he hurt us. You tried to pretend like nothing was going on. You wanted us to see this perfect family. We knew all along. No, he never hit you. Yes, we knew about the other women. We heard you all arguing when you thought we were sleeping. Then he started to hurt us. While in therapy at the facility, I learned that we felt how you felt. We did not want to tell anyone. We held everything in until we eventually were unhappy that we made a pack to kill ourselves so that we would die together. I did not want to leave Mia here to deal with abuse, and she did not want to leave me here. We didn't die, Mama. We are here. We are happy now. Thank you for believing us. Thank you for loving us. Now, it's time for you to be happy. You will be an even greater mother if you are happy." She got up from the chair, kissed me on my cheek, and said, "I love you, Mama. Good night."

My baby had me crying. I wiped my tears. There was God using my child to speak to me again.

Will

The only time I asked my mother to watch my children or when Kim asked if the girls could stay with Allison was when she and I needed alone time! If we were not alone, we would all be together. If we were not at my house, we were at Kim's house. When school started back, I enjoyed attending games to watch the twins cheer and dance. If not at little league games and cheer, we were cheering the twins on in soccer, volleyball, tennis, or softball games! They were very athletic and talented. If there was no game, we were out bowling, skating, or traveling. We traveled to different cities to theme parks, vacations, and even camping! Our children loved one another's company. I kept my end of the deal I made with Mya. As it got closer to their sweet sixteen, I began to teach them how to drive. They learned in the Camaro. Just as Mya said, Kim was not going about her cars!

The twins maintained their 3.8 and 3.75-grade point averages and were able to pass the written driver's test to receive their permits. A couple of days before their party, they took the driver's test. They both passed! They were legal to drive! Kim and I both helped with their surprise sweet sixteen birthday party! They were so happy when we removed their blindfolds and they saw two cars. They were different girls! The cars matched their personality. Mia was given a red Volkswagen Beetle, and Mya was given a black charger. They were ready! I was excited for them! They deserved it.

Kim

Even though our children were doing well, and we were doing well, Will and I decided to take phase II of our counseling. Phase II dealt more with the entire family. He wanted to make sure he and his children as a unit were healthy, and I wanted to do the same with my girls. It was the best decision we could have made. His children enjoyed it. I enjoyed it. There were times when we cried together, and I am quite sure he and his children cried at times as well. There were times we had to visit places that we did not want to visit again, but we tackled it like champs! We were not the only families participating in phase II. Others that were in our original group counseling session joined with their families. After we successfully completed the phase, we were scheduled to have a graduation and picnic. The graduation was for the parents that completed phase I, and the picnic was for the families that completed phase II. The facilitator and family therapist encouraged us to invite our friends and family.

The mutual friends that Will and I shared did attend. Our families were there as well. At the graduation, each group from phase I was to come to the stage and share information they learned about their partner and highlight successful moments in their treatment. Will had two partners. We each had to go with him. He shared what he learned about his other partner first and then began to share what he learned about me.

Will

I ended up in Crestview because I was searching for a pediatrician for my children. I began to do my research. I learned the number one ranked pediatrician in all of the United States of America was in a small town called Crestview. I moved here because my children needed the best. Child protective services felt it was best that I attended counseling while I was here with everything that happened to my children. So, I did. I had no idea that I would be sitting in the room with the number one-ranked pediatrician in all of the United States of America. I had no idea she would be my support partner. She was very difficult to work with at first. Our facilitator suggested we do some things our partner liked. Well, she never talked! We shared friends! She was different around them. I liked her with our friends better than I did at the group session! I then remembered the article I found about her. I remember seeing the fun facts section about her. I used the article to find things to do with her. As we did things, I learned more about her, and she learned more about me. I learned she is a wonderful mother to her twin daughters, she loves her career and treats all patients with the same love, she is a great supporter, she can cook, Italian food is her favorite, she loves chocolate ice cream, she is the best spades partner, she is hilarious, you can count on her to say whatever she wants to say, most of all, she is a godly woman. I learned I was attracted to her. I learned she is beautiful on the outside but even more beautiful on the inside. She's a tough chocolate chip, but even I can make her melt. My children love her. I adore her girls.

Kim

I was blushing. He then said, "Speaking of our children, can you all come up here, please."

He was up to something. My girls started smiling from ear to ear. I knew they were in on whatever he was doing. I watched as our facilitator came to the stage carrying small posters. She was in on it too. As each of them walked onto the stage, she handed them a poster. He took me by my hand and placed me in front of him, facing each of them. The facilitator put the microphone in front of Ryleigh first. My girl flipped over her sign, and it read *Mama Kim.*

She then said, "You have been more than Dr. Kim to me."

Junior flipped over his sign, and it read, *Can I call you that too?*

He said, "You now have a son."

Mya took the mic and flipped over her sign. It read, Happiness is the Key.

She then said, "God has given you the key, Mama. Use it."

Mia then took the mic from her and flipped over her sign. It read, Praying Partner.

Mia said, "Mama when I woke up at the

hospital, Will was standing next to my bed praying for me. Allow him to be there for you to help you pray when things get rough from this point on."

I couldn't stop my tears if I tried. They all then said in unison, "Turn Around, Mama."

I turned around. More tears flowed at the sight of Will kneeling on one knee with a white box in his hand that held a diamond ring.

"Kimberly, I love you. Will you allow me to be your husband? Will you allow me to love you and your girls the way you all are supposed to be loved? Will you be the mother my children need? Will you be the wife I've never had but always dreamed of having?" The kids then gathered around him.

Junior said, "Will you marry us?"

Ryleigh said, "Will you be my mommy?"

Mya and Mia said, "You deserve to say what your heart feels."

I then said, "Yes, I will allow you to be my husband. I will allow you to love me and my girls. I the way we are supposed to be loved. I will be the mother your children need. I will be the wife you have never had but always dreamed of having. Yes! Yes! Yes!"

He slid the ring onto my finger. It was the perfect fit. He gently pulled me in his arms and gave me a peck on my lips that led to me giving him a peck that ended in us sharing a long engaging kiss.

THE END

About The Author

Latoya Geter

Author LaToya C. Geter has ranked #1 among Amazon's Best Sellers in African American Christian Fiction. She has been writing since the 5th grade. She also enjoys writing poetry. She is the daughter of the late Romunda Owens and granddaughter of the late Betty Williams. God blessed her with her dad, Kirk Owens. She has been blessed to have her spiritual father and inspiration behind Christian fiction writing, Reginal Wesley Alexander Sr. When she is not writing she is basking in her femininity or kicking and punching as a third-degree black belt in taekwondo. She loves being in the presence of her fiancé and soon to be husband Deddrick. She is a fur mom to her dogs Ace and Charlie and her guinea pig, Mannie. She is an active and financial member of Sigma Gamma Rho Sorority Inc.

Books In This Series

The Recipe Of A Godly Woman
The series begins with the story of how Audrey met Daniel. Audrey has three friends. Lauren, Kim and Allison. Each of the women have their story. The women experience trials and tribulations but each are renewed and fall in love.

The Recipe Of A Godly Woman

A single pastor moves to a segregated town to lead a church deeply rooted in sin. Without knowledge of the sin, he begins to casually date the church clerk. While attempting to bring both sides of the town together, he meets a single mother filled with anger, betrayal, hurt and secrets; and finds himself losing sight of God's direction for him. A life-threatening storm destroys the church and the town, but opens his heart and leads him to the true woman of God.

The Recipe Of A Godly Woman 2

When Pastor Reynolds and Audrey start to live

their life as a married couple, challenges begin. Audrey learns her son taken from her at birth has actually lived in the next town over for years. She learns her mother is still keeping secrets from her. Her biological father is alive and willing to have a relationship with her. Someone is out to destroy her business and life. Pastor Reynolds just may know the person who is out to destroy his wife. Is it a man or his ex-girlfriend who suffers from mental illness? Will Audrey be able to take on the challenges, be a mother and wife all while being attacked over and over again? When Audrey finally comes face to face with her enemy will she take that opportunity to get revenge or allow God to come in?

The Recipe Of A Godly Woman 3

Dr. Cornelius Fairbanks is the new single emergency room physician in Crestview. Lauren, Audrey's best friend, has been keeping a secret. Due to her frequent visits to the ER, Dr. Fairbanks discovers Lauren's secret. She has the same secret a person dear to his heart kept hidden until death. With more visits to the ER, the secret is at risk of getting out. Cornelius gives Lauren his number to call him for help. Her calls of distress results in him coming to her rescue each time. Coming to her rescue leads to him taking her to the one place where he knows he can keep her safe without exposing her secret, his home. The nights spent at his home are nights of security and peace in his arms. While trying to keep her secret and save her, Cornelius learns more about her, and Lauren discovers more about him. The two become attracted to one another, and emotions begin to take over. Cornelius cannot save Lauren from the last life-threatening admission into the hospital because she is married. When she believes her marriage can work, her husband promises to end her life if she ever returns to Cornelius. Lauren leaves Crestview without telling anyone. She finds herself going back on a journey of forgiveness. After forgiving everyone who hurt her from childhood into adulthood, she is faced with explaining herself to one person. Will Cornelius hear her out or shut her out forever? Will God restore her marriage or open a new door to true love?

Made in the USA
Coppell, TX
11 December 2022